OUTB

Marriage is their mission!

From bad boys to powerful, passionate protectors! Three tycoons from the Outback rescue their brides-to-be....

Meet Ric, Mitch and Johnny—once rebellious teenagers, they survived the Outback to become best friends and formidable tycoons. Now these sexy city slickers must return to the Outback to face a new challenge: claiming their brides....

This month, it's sexy lawyer Mitch Tyler's turn!

• May 2004:
The Outback Marriage Ransom (#2391)

• July 2004:
The Outback Wedding Takeover (#2403)

• November 2004:
The Outback Bridal Rescue (#2427)

Emma Darcy is the award-winning Australian author of over eighty novels for Harlequin Presents®.
Her intensely emotional stories have gripped readers around the world. She's sold nearly 60 million copies of her books worldwide and has won enthusiastic praise.

"Emma Darcy delivers a spicy love story... a fiery conflict and a hot sensuality."
—*Romantic Times*

Dear Reader,

To me, there has always been something immensely intriguing about bad boys who've made good. With every possible disadvantage in their background, what was it that lifted them beyond it, that gave them the driving force to achieve, to soar to the heights of their chosen fields, becoming much more than survivors... shining stars?

In OUTBACK KNIGHTS I've explored the lives of three city boys who ended up in juvenile court and were sent to an Outback sheep station to work through their sentences. There, at Gundamurra, isolated from the influences that had overwhelmed them in the past and under the supervision and care of a shrewd mentor, Patrick Maguire, the boys' lives became set on different paths as they learned how their individual strengths—their passions—can be used constructively instead of destructively.

But the big unanswered need is love. Even at the top it's lonely.

And it seemed to me beautifully fitting that as these boys had been rescued, so should they—as men—rescue the women who will give them love. I think there are times when all of us want to be rescued—to be cared for, protected, understood, made to feel safe. It's not that we can't manage independently, but, oh, for a knight in shining armor who will fight and slay our dragons with a passionate intensity that makes us melt! Here they are—Ric Donato, Mitch Tyler and Johnny Ellis: OUTBACK KNIGHTS!

With love,

Emma Darcy

Emma Darcy

THE OUTBACK WEDDING TAKEOVER

OUTBACK KNIGHTS

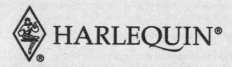

HARLEQUIN®

TORONTO • NEW YORK • LONDON
AMSTERDAM • PARIS • SYDNEY • HAMBURG
STOCKHOLM • ATHENS • TOKYO • MILAN • MADRID
PRAGUE • WARSAW • BUDAPEST • AUCKLAND

ISBN 0-373-12403-1

THE OUTBACK WEDDING TAKEOVER

First North American Publication 2004.

www.eHarlequin.com

Printed in U.S.A.

PROLOGUE

THE plane was heading down to a red dirt airstrip. Apart from the cluster of buildings that marked the sheep station of Gundamurra, there was no other habitation in sight between here and the horizon—a huge empty landscape dotted with scrubby trees.

'Wish I had my camera,' Ric Donato murmured.

Mitch Tyler frowned over the other boy's words. Apparently the stark visual impact of the place didn't intimidate Ric. But then the guy had been copped joyriding in a stolen Porsche. He probably got off on wide-open spaces, while Mitch had always been happiest with a book in his hands. No local library here to tap into.

'The middle of nowhere,' he muttered dispiritedly. 'I'm beginning to think I made the wrong choice.'

'Nah,' Johnny Ellis drawled. 'Anything's better than being locked up. At least we can breathe out here.'

'What? Dust?' Mitch mocked.

The plane landed, kicking up a cloud of it.

'Welcome to the great Australian Outback,' the cop escorting them said derisively. 'And just remember...if you three city smart-arses want to survive, there's nowhere to run.'

All three of them ignored him. They were sixteen. Regardless of what life threw at them, they were going to survive. And Johnny had it right, Mitch thought. Six months working on a sheep station had to be better than a year in a juvenile jail.

It was half the time, for a start, and there were only two other guys with him, not a horde of criminals who would have established a pecking order. Mitch hated bullies with a passion. He'd learnt how to look after himself. No-one touched him anymore. But he sure didn't want to be incarcerated with a mob of power pushers.

He hoped the owner of this place wasn't some kind of little Hitler, exploiting the justice system to get a free labour force. Mitch decided he'd work out for himself what was fair and challenge anything that wasn't.

What had the judge said at the sentencing? Something about getting back to ground values. A program that would teach them what real life was about. Wouldn't teach him a damned thing about *real life,* Mitch had thought at the time. He'd majored in *real life,* ever since his father had walked out on his crippled wife, leaving him and his sister to look after their mother. The lion's share of that had fallen to Jenny, who'd only been eleven years old to his eight when their father had deserted them. Not that he'd been much help anyway, getting drunk every night, drowning his sorrows instead of facing up to them. A coward. That was what his father had been. A contemptible coward.

But not as contemptible as the guy who'd date-raped Jenny.

At least Mitch had had the satisfaction of facing that bastard with what he'd done.

There she'd been, all excited about being invited to a swish party, finally getting into a bit of social life, and to be treated like a disposable piece of meat...

He was glad he'd given that piece of slime a beating he'd remember for a long time. It might be primitive justice, and against the law, but better than letting him get away with it, no justice at all. Jenny had been too traumatised to press charges against him. The silver-spoon heir to a fortune would probably have got off anyway, with his mega-wealthy family having the power and influence to get anything excused.

Mitch felt no remorse over what he'd done. None whatsoever. Though he was sorry he wouldn't be at home to help for the next six months.

The plane taxied back to where a man—the owner?—was waiting beside a four-wheel drive Land Rover. Big man—broad-shouldered, barrel-chested, craggy weathered face, iron-grey hair. Had to be over fifty but still looking tough and formidable. Not someone to buck in a hurry, Mitch decided, though size didn't automatically command his respect.

'John Wayne rides again,' he mocked to cover his unease with the situation.

'No horse,' Johnny remarked with a grin.

Mitch found himself smiling back.

It looked like Johnny Ellis would provide some comic relief if life got grim here. He seemed to have the kind of affable nature that would avoid violence if it was avoidable, though even at sixteen his physique was big enough and strong enough to match anyone in a punch-up if forced into it.

Johnny and Ric were street kids. No family. And no doubt they'd worked out ways of looking after themselves. Mitch figured Johnny specialised in being everyone's mate. He had friendly hazel eyes, a ready grin, and sun-streaked brown hair that tended to flop over his forehead. He'd been caught dealing in marijuana, though he swore it was only to musicians who'd get it from someone else anyway.

Ric Donato was a very different kettle of fish. He had an intensity about him that could make him dangerous, Mitch thought. Was he a thief because he wanted too much, too obsessively? He seemed to have a very single-minded passion for the girl he'd stolen the Porsche for, wanting to match up to her rich life.

Mitch imagined that most girls would get a thrill out of Ric, just by being the focus of his attention. The guy had sex appeal in spades—mad, bad and dangerous, well-built without being hunky, and strikingly handsome in a very macho Italian way—black curly hair, almost black eyes, olive skin, and a face that Michelangelo might have carved for its masculine beauty. Perversely enough, the guy didn't seem to have tickets on himself at all. Like he'd been hit too many times to believe he'd been handed anything to feel good about.

Mitch felt okay with himself. Angry at what had been dealt out to his family, but okay with the person he was. He didn't have Ric's good looks but he was presentable enough—on the lean side but not a weakling, taller than most guys his age, and having blue eyes with almost black hair seemed to impress some girls.

Mitch would prefer them to be more impressed by the smart brain that had got him labelled as a nerd before he took up boxing at the local boys' club. He'd never understood why using his intelligence earned scornful remarks from the jocks. Anyhow, he wasn't called a nerd or a weed any more. He might not be liked but he'd made damned sure he was respected.

The plane came to a halt.

The cop told them to get their duffle-bags from under the back seats. A few minutes later he was leading them out to a way of life which was far, far removed from anything the three of them had known before.

The initial introduction had Mitch instantly tensing up.

'Here are your boys, Mister Maguire. Straight off the city streets for you to whip into shape.'

The big old man—and he sure was big close up—gave the cop a steely look. 'That's not how we do things out here.' The words were softly spoken but they carried a confident authority that scorned any need for bully-boy tactics.

He nodded to the three of them, offering a measure of respect. 'I'm Patrick Maguire. Welcome to Gundamurra. In the Aboriginal language, that means ''Good day''. I hope you will all eventually feel it was a good day when you first set foot on my place.'

Mitch felt reassured by this little speech. It had a

welcoming ring to it, no punishment intended. As long as they were treated fairly, Mitch was prepared to cope with whatever work was thrown at them. He mostly lived in his mind, anyway.

'And you are…?' Patrick Maguire held out a massive hand that looked suspiciously like a bone-cruncher.

'Mitch Tyler,' he answered, thrusting his own hand out in defiant challenge.

'Good to meet you, Mitch.'

A normal hand-shake, no attempt to dominate.

Johnny's hand came out with no hesitation. 'Johnny Ellis. Good to meet you, Mister Maguire.' Big smile to the old man, pouring out the charm. Getting onside fast was Johnny.

A weighing look in the steely grey gaze, plus a hint of amusement. No-one's fool, Mitch thought, impressed by the shrewd intelligence of the man and watching him keenly as he moved on to Ric who looked every bit as keyed up as Mitch had been.

'Ric Donato.' It was a flat introduction, strained of any telltale emotion. Ric took the offered hand, feeling the strength in it, seeming to test what it might mean to him.

'Ready to go?' the old man asked.

'Yeah. I'm ready.' Aggression in this reply.

Ready to take on the whole damned world if he had to, Mitch interpreted. Ric Donato might not have tickets on himself but he sure had a huge chip on his shoulder. Mitch wondered if Patrick Maguire would somehow manage to remove it while they were here.

Would he also be able to dig under Johnny's genial facade and discover what made Johnny tick?

The knowing grey eyes swept back to Mitch and he felt himself bristling defensively. Did this old man of the land have anything to teach him? Only about sheep, Mitch thought mockingly…yet six months was a long time, and for all he knew right now, he might end up feeling it was a 'good day' when he'd first set foot on Gundamurra.

CHAPTER ONE

Eighteen years later...

THE iron composure of the woman in the witness stand finally cracked. Mitch knew his cross-examination had been merciless. At his lethal best. And totally justified in his mind. This woman had shown no mercy to her son who'd begged his mother for help which had been steadfastly refused, and not even his suicide had softened her heart toward her bereft daughter-in-law. He watched her break into weeping and felt no sympathy at all.

She wasn't weeping over her lost son.

She wasn't weeping over the torment he'd suffered.

She was weeping because she'd been faced with her own monstrous ego that had branded her son a failure for not living up to what *she* had required from him.

And now it was going to cost her, not only in having her character stripped bare in public, but also in an appropriate financial settlement for the cast-off daughter-in-law and her baby son.

His opposing counsel, Harriet Lowell, who also happened to be Mitch's recently excised partner in bed, requested a recess and the judge decided it was close enough to the lunch break to take it now, court to be resumed at two o'clock.

Harriet threw Mitch a dirty look as she moved to assist her client from the witness stand. He returned a steely gaze that promised more of the same after lunch if there was no agreement to the settlement he was demanding on behalf of his client.

Harriet could spit chips at how he was handling this case but he was going to win it hands down. Justice would be served. And he was glad it had come to this—payment in more than dollars. People who gave pain should feel it themselves. The trick was to find what actually hurt them, make them reconsider their position. And keep it all under a legal umbrella.

Use the system to get justice.

That's what Patrick Maguire had taught him.

It was a good system if it was used as it was meant to be used. Patrick had been right about that. Mitch had been studying the law ever since he'd left Gundamurra—eighteen years—orchestrating what was necessary to get his own juvenile conviction for assault set aside so he could enter the profession, working his way up to becoming a barrister with a formidable reputation for winning the cases he took on.

He believed in them. That was what made the difference. He never took on a case unless he believed he was fighting for right, and then he gave it everything he could bring to it. Harriet saw the law as a chess game—moves and counter-moves—but to Mitch the chessboard was always black and white, and he wasn't interested in playing black.

His clerk met him outside the courtroom, handing him a message from Ric Donato. He couldn't make lunch today. Disappointing. Mitch always enjoyed meeting up with Ric. And Johnny. Although their lives had travelled very different paths since their time at Gundamurra, the three of them had remained good friends over the years.

They shared the common bond of Patrick Maguire's influence in setting them on the paths they'd chosen—each to their own bent. And they understood where each other was coming from and why. Not too many people ever achieved that kind of understanding.

It came from living together in constant proximity for six months. There were few distractions in the outback. It was a place for talking, chewing over things, reflecting on what had meaning and what didn't, sharing each other's visions of the world. And dreams.

Ric had become an award-winning photo-journalist—amazing stuff he'd shot with his camera. Retired from the job now and running an international photographic agency. Very successfully.

Johnny was a star with his country music, currently touring the U.S.—a millionaire many times over with most of his recordings going platinum.

Mitch was the only one whose chosen career kept him in Australia. The halls of justice called to him and Sydney was his city. Still, it was great to catch up with the others when they were in town. He wondered what had caused Ric to miss their lunch today—had to be some business problem.

'Cancel the booking at the restaurant,' he instructed

his clerk. 'I'll buy some sandwiches, eat in the park, get some fresh air.'

If he couldn't have Ric's company to dilute the cold nastiness of this case, he'd prefer to be outdoors, soaking up some sunshine.

Sitting in the park reminded Mitch of his own mother—the countless times he'd pushed her wheelchair to the small park near where they'd lived at Surry Hills. Every Saturday and Sunday if it was fine. Fresh air and sunshine, being outside, watching other people, spending time together, giving Jenny a break so she felt free to go and do her own thing—which was what his mother had always encouraged for both of them, hating the idea of her disability holding them back from pursuing goals of their own.

She hadn't tried to rule the lives of her children, not like the woman he'd just pilloried on the witness stand, meting out punishment when her son hadn't measured up to her predetermined mould for him. If anything, his own mother had been too self-effacing, not even wanting to ask for what was her rightful due.

It was good that she'd lived long enough to see him called to the bar. She'd been very proud of that achievement. And she'd seen Jenny married to a good guy, too. Both her children doing well for themselves. If he ever had children himself…well, that wasn't going to happen any time soon.

He'd dallied with the idea of marrying Harriet. They shared the same profession. She was a smart, witty woman and he'd generally enjoyed her company. Enjoyed the sex with her, too. Until he'd found out she was also having sex with one of the judges, laughing it off as simply a strategy to give her an edge in court. Winning was what Harriet was about. Winning at all costs. She'd probably thought winning him would be a feather in her cap. She'd certainly been angling for marriage.

No way now, Mitch thought. If he ever married, he'd want honesty in the relationship. Loyalty, too. As for love…well, Harriet had engaged his mind, but had she ever really engaged his heart? Mitch wasn't sure what love was between a man and a woman. Attraction, yes. A sexual high, yes. But love…maybe he'd become too disciplined in controlling emotion to feel a deep abiding passion for a woman.

He strolled back to the court house, gearing himself up for another competitive round with Harriet who'd no doubt be objecting to every tack he took with her client. His clerk met him on the steps with another message—this one from Ric's executive assistant in Sydney, a woman by the name of Kathryn Ledger, asking him to return her call on a matter of urgency.

Was Ric in trouble?

A broken lunch appointment, no excuse given.

Now an urgent call from his office.

Mitch glanced at his watch. Still ten minutes before he was due in court. He whipped out his mobile phone, retreated down the steps for a quick bit of privacy and called the number written on the message slip.

'Kathryn Ledger,' came the brisk response.

'Mitch Tyler. I don't have much time. What's the problem?'

'In a nutshell…Ric received photographic evidence

this morning that a woman he knows is a battered wife. He went straight to her home and took her out of the situation. He's flown her off somewhere in Johnny Ellis's plane.'

'Good God!' Mitch muttered in disbelief.

'The husband was having her watched by a private investigator who lost their trail at our basement car park when Ric switched cars.' The incredible tale went on. 'Her husband has since turned up at our office, harassing the staff for information. I gave him the name of the restaurant where you and Ric were supposed to meet for lunch, but he's bound to come back when he doesn't find Ric there. My instructions were to call you if there was trouble.'

'A woman he knew?' Mitch queried.

'He called her Lara Seymour and said they went back a long way.'

Ric's Lara? From when he was sixteen?

Mitch's mind boggled.

Could a youthful passion last this long?

Stealing a Porsche to impress a girl was one thing. Stealing a married woman from her husband—eighteen years later!—was one hell of a leap.

'But the name isn't Lara Seymour now,' the informing voice went on. 'It's Lara Chappel...married to Gary Chappel, son of Victor Chappel. You know who I mean?'

Gary Chappel!

Mitch was momentarily poleaxed by shock.

'Mr Tyler? The Chappel medical clinic and nursing home empire? We're talking big money and power here. And we've got trouble.'

Mitch's trapped breath hissed out as his mind clicked to action stations. 'I know exactly what you mean, Ms Ledger. Do you still have this photographic evidence?'

'Yes. Five copies in the safe.'

'I'll be sending two security men to escort you to my chambers. Do not leave your office until they arrive. Bring one copy of the photograph with you. Once you are safely in my chambers, wait in my private office for me. I'll join you as soon as I'm free. I cannot emphasise enough…follow these instructions to the letter, Ms Ledger. Believe me, you have big trouble.'

'Thank you, Mr Tyler. Rest assured I'll follow your advice.'

'Good!'

Efficient and sensible, Mitch thought as he hurried back to his clerk. As she should be, given her executive position in Ric's business. All the same, he was impressed by her quick summary of the situation and her no-quibbling response to the course of action he'd outlined.

He told his clerk what he wanted done, adding, 'This is urgent business. Get the security men there pronto, and tell them Ms Ledger is carrying merchandise that is invaluable.'

Definitely *invaluable,* Mitch thought with grim satisfaction. Legal evidence against Gary Chappel! No way could that bastard wriggle out of this one. Or buy his way out. Not with Mitch Tyler having a controlling hand.

Harriet signalled him aside just as he was about to

enter the courtroom. Even with a barrister's wig covering her silky blond hair, she still looked beautiful—flawless creamy skin, her full-lipped sensuous mouth painted a glossy red, a fine aristocratic nose breathing fire while her big grey eyes smoked with angry frustration.

'Where have you been?' she demanded.

Not at *her* beck and call any more.

He raised a mocking eyebrow. 'Out. Is your client ready to settle?'

'She's ready to deal.'

'The only deal on the table is what I nominated from the beginning.'

'She won't come at that.'

'Then I'll see you both in court.'

Harriet reached out and grabbed the sleeve of his robe, halting him. 'This is blackmail, Mitch.'

'No. It's exposure.'

Which was what Gary Chappel deserved, too.

Though it probably wouldn't work out that way.

Better to hold the sword over his head if the aim was to keep everyone free of trouble.

'You're painting this black and white, not accepting any greys. And there are greys,' Harriet insisted vehemently.

'Then prove it to the jury.'

'You know damned well you've got their sympathy.'

'I wonder why.'

With that mocking retort he pulled his robe free of her grasp and headed into the courtroom, prepared to fight on but suspecting he wouldn't have to. That little contretemps had sounded like a last-ditch effort to get him to bend a little, win something for her client, which, of course, would be a face-saving exercise for Harriet. Total defeat didn't sit well with her. Never would. Greys suited her better.

No sooner was everyone settled in the courtroom than Harriet made the request to approach the bench. In very short order, Mitch was informed that Harriet's client had conceded and full settlement was agreed upon. The case was over, bar the paperwork.

Normally Mitch would have felt enormously gratified by this result but he found himself impatient with having to tie up all the ends, deal with the media, and see his client off with the courtesy due to her. This fight had been won. Gary Chappel was now in the antagonist's corner and Mitch's mind was already occupied with the fight ahead.

Kathryn Ledger was no more than a name and a voice to him. He thought of her only as a source, bringing him the ammunition he'd use to attack. That she was also a woman held no relevance at all until he entered his private office and came face-to-face with her.

CHAPTER TWO

IT WAS like a bolt of electric energy charging into the room. Kathryn felt as though she'd been zapped off the chair she'd been sitting on, her body lifting onto her feet, straightening up, instinctively meeting the force of the man head on, while staring at him in wide-eyed shock.

This was Mitch Tyler?

A barrister?

She'd always thought of barristers as rather lofty and effete academics in fusty wigs, full of their own self-importance. Yet here she was, faced with a dynamic entity who literally bristled with masculinity, so much so her knees felt weak. And her heart was fluttering.

Tall, dark and handsome, but not like Ric Donato. Not like Ric at all. Any woman would call her boss drop-dead gorgeous, but this man didn't come out of any romantic mould. Power was the only word that came to Kathryn's dazed mind. He had a strong square jaw, very firmly delineated mouth, a sharp triangular shaped nose, straight black brows, and beneath them, stunning blue eyes that burned straight into Kathryn's like twin lasers, totally transfixing her.

She stared at him and he stared right back at her. Kathryn couldn't gather wits enough to say a word. The mutual stare went on so long, she began to wonder if he doubted her identity, though surely his clerk would have told him she was waiting in here where he'd told her to wait.

Mitch was thinking Ric must be mad. He had *this* woman right under his nose and he ran off with someone else?

She was like Tinkerbell…magic…a pixie face with those wonderful green eyes and the gamine hairstyle, like a flyaway cap of burnished copper, a lovely pouty mouth that was made for kissing, an hourglass figure poured into a curve-hugging green suit, the skirt delectably short enough to show off long, shapely legs…how could Ric be immune to such gut-tugging femininity? Mitch was struggling to remember this was a professional visit.

'Mr Tyler…?'

Her voice sounded husky, uncertain…and incredibly sexy.

'Mitch,' he said forcefully, deciding Kathryn Ledger was not his client and he didn't have to keep a professional distance. She was here on Ric's behalf. And Lara Chappel's. He propelled himself forward, offering his hand. 'Good to meet you, Kathryn.' Lovely name. Rolled off his tongue as though he'd been saying it for centuries.

'Mitch,' she repeated, looking at him wonderingly as her hand slipped into his.

The top of her head only came up to his chin so her face was tilted up. There were sparkly gold specks around the rim of her green irises like an explosion of fireworks. Her mouth was still slightly parted from having spoken his name and Mitch had to fight the urge to bend down and taste it. Her hand was soft, dainty, and he hung onto it because it was the only touch he could sensibly allow himself at this point. They'd barely met.

'No trouble coming here?' he asked, pushing his mind to get back on track—the whole purpose of her presence in his office.

'No. Thank you for the escorts.' A swift little smile. 'They certainly made me feel safe.'

'Good!' He smiled back, feeling a wild joy in having protected this woman. And he'd go on protecting her, whatever it took. 'You've brought the photo?'

'Yes. In my bag.'

She nodded to a many-zippered beige handbag resting by the chair she'd been sitting on. Mitch reluctantly released her hand, freeing her to get the critical photo for him. Losing the physical link made him realise how possessive he was feeling toward Kathryn Ledger—amazingly so. He couldn't recall any other woman ever having such an impact on him.

He watched her lift the bag onto his desk as he mentally examined the primitive instincts she stirred. Control was second nature to him. Only once in his life had he completely lost it, wanting to beat Jenny's rapist to a pulp, and he might well have done so if he hadn't been forcibly restrained.

Control the anger and channel the energy into more effective strategies, Patrick had advised. But this... what he was feeling now with Kathryn Ledger...was completely outside Mitch's experience and he couldn't find any control mechanisms for it. His entire body seemed to be buzzing with excitement.

Her left hand moved to open a zipper on the bag. It was like a punch in the heart, seeing the ring on her third finger. A ring with a flashy solitaire diamond. An engagement ring!

She was taken.

Another man had already claimed her as his.

Anger smashed through the shock. It wasn't right. It couldn't be right. He'd fight to…

No!

Mitch shook his head clear of the crazy surge of testosterone, enforcing reason. Kathryn Ledger had willingly given herself to someone else. Someone she obviously wanted to marry. Her choice was made. And, of course, Ric had respected it. She wasn't available to him any more than she was available to Mitch.

Checkmate!

He had to back off.

Never mind that it felt wrong.

She had come to him for help. Nothing more. He had to get his mind focused on the job and forget everything else.

Kathryn was trying desperately to get herself together. It didn't help that her hand was still tingling from Mitch Tyler's touch, that her legs felt shaky, and she could barely concentrate on opening her bag and extracting the telling photograph. She felt as though she'd been knocked completely out of kilter.

For a moment there, she'd even been wondering what it might be like if Mitch Tyler kissed her.

Jeremy—her partner for the past year!—had been totally blotted out of her mind. The reason for being here in these legal chambers had been lost, too. It was as though she'd been caught up in some magnetic force-field that shut out everything else but the man holding her hand, and she was still quivering inside from the unbelievably strong tug of his attraction.

Her fingers closed over the photograph and she took a deep breath before turning to hand it to him. It was a relief that his gaze instantly fastened on the image of Lara and Gary Chappel, giving her more time to recover her composure. Better still when he stepped away from her, moving around to the other side of his desk, putting considerable distance between them, enough distance to ease the tightness in her chest.

'Thank you,' he said, flicking a look at her as he gestured to the chair she'd vacated. 'Please sit down again.'

She grabbed her bag off the desk and gratefully retreated even further, settling herself before risking another glance at him. He'd sat down, too, occupying the big leather chair behind his desk, studying the photograph she'd given him, his straight black brows lowered in a frown.

His dark hair was also straight, very thick and cut short in graduated layers to stay neat. He had neat ears, as well, almost no lobes like her own, but curved around the top, not pointy. He wouldn't have been teased about having pixie ears when he was a kid. She couldn't imagine anyone ever teasing Mitch Tyler. One look from those powerful blue eyes…

A convulsive little shiver ran down her spine. He had to be dynamite in a courtroom. She wondered how Ric had come to know him. They looked to be about the same age—mid-thirties—yet she couldn't see how their lives would have touched. As far as she knew, her boss had not gone through university. Maybe somewhere in his years as a photo-journalist he'd sought legal assistance. Whatever…Ric Donato trusted this man and Kathryn could see why he would. In any kind of fight, she'd want Mitch Tyler on her side.

He jackknifed forward, picked up the telephone from his desk, made a call, still frowning as he waited for a response which came within a few moments. 'Patrick, it's Mitch. Have you heard from Ric today?'

The reply must have been negative because he quickly ran on, 'I think he's heading your way. Took Johnny's plane out. If you hear from him would you please let me know?'

Another pause, a grimace, then, 'He left me with a problem and I'd appreciate more instructions. If he calls you, tell him to call me. Okay?'

Phone down. He knew Johnny Ellis, too, Kathryn thought, and all three men were obviously connected to this Patrick whom Mitch had just called.

'Ric didn't tell me where he was going,' she offered.

The laser-sharp eyes bored into hers again. 'He wouldn't. Not in these circumstances. Fill me in on the whole story, Kathryn, as much as you know.'

His gaze alone seemed to be picking at her brain. Kathryn felt constrained to remember every little detail in case it was vitally important. 'You know Ric's business,' she started.

'Brokering photographs to all forms of media around the world,' he rapped out, tapping the one he'd now laid on the desk in front of him. 'This one was e-mailed in?'

'Yes. Taken at the airport. Dated yesterday. We were checking through the computer file this morning…'

'What time was it when Ric saw this?'

'About nine-thirty. Normally we don't deal in shots that might cause people problems. I was about to delete this one when Ric stopped me. He asked me to print it, give him a copy, put five more copies in the office safe and buy the copyright from the photographer so no-one else could print it. He said he didn't care how much it cost…just get it.'

Mitch nodded thoughtfully. 'Did you acquire the copyright?'

'Yes. After Ric left. Which he did as soon as I'd printed out his copy. He took it with him. I didn't know what he was going to do. He simply said he and Lara Chappel…Lara Seymour…went way back and she wouldn't want that photo published. I felt…' She hesitated, wondering if she should colour the facts with her feelings or not.

'Tell me,' Mitch encouraged.

She sighed. 'All this was out of character. That photo got to him personally. In a big way. It wasn't normal business, if you know what I mean.'

It evoked a wry little smile. 'I guess we all have moments that aren't…normal.'

A flood of heat whooshed up her neck and scorched her cheeks. Kathryn couldn't remember the last time she had blushed. She was thirty years old, a successful career woman, adept at handling all sorts of people and situations. Yet here was embarrassing proof of how *abnormal* her reaction was to this man. Was it horribly obvious that he'd put her in such a spin, even her blood temperature was affected?

Stick to the facts, girl, she berated herself. Best to steer right away from feelings, because she was in a high state of confusion about her own.

'It was just past eleven when Ric called me from his car,' she went on briskly. 'He said he was heading back to the office, should be there in ten minutes. He had Lara Chappel with him and he needed my help. He instructed me to tell my secretary I'd be away for a couple of hours at a business meeting with a mag-azine editor—nothing unusual about that—and meet him in the basement car park with my bag and car keys.'

'You didn't question what help Ric wanted?'

Kathryn shrugged. 'He's my boss.'

'How did he sound?'

'Very much in command.'

Mitch Tyler nodded. 'Ric has worked in war zones. He'd keep his head.'

Kathryn didn't know if Mitch was reassuring her or himself. Certainly the familiar way he spoke of Ric's past suggested a long and close friendship.

'So you were there waiting for him when he drove into the basement car park,' he prompted.

'Yes. Ric said they'd been followed by a grey sedan—male driver wearing a baseball cap and sunglasses—bound to be hanging around outside since there was no entry to the private car park without an official identification card. He wanted me to drive him and Lara Chappel to Bankstown Airport. They got into my car and scrunched down in their seats while I drove out, and they stayed down until I could assure them we weren't being followed by the pursuit vehicle.'

'Did Lara Chappel say anything to you?'

'Not until we arrived at the airport. She simply did whatever Ric told her to.'

'How did she appear to you? Her reactions to what was going on?'

Kathryn paused, wanting to be accurate in her impressions. 'Nervous, frightened, distracted,' she answered slowly.

Mitch cocked his head to one side, a musing expression on his face. 'Did it occur to you that you could be accused of assisting in an unlawful abduction?'

Kathryn was shocked into protesting. 'It was a getaway, not an abduction. Lara Chappel was willingly following Ric's lead.'

He leaned forward and tapped the photograph on the desk. 'Ric might have used this for leverage.'

'He wouldn't do that.'

The blue eyes glittered mockingly. 'How can you tell what a man will do...when he wants a woman very badly?'

His gaze slid down to her mouth and Kathryn found herself holding her breath while her heart skittered, reacting to what felt like a simmering passion aimed directly at her. Was he just projecting what he thought Ric might feel toward Lara Chappel? Was a clever barrister a brilliant actor, as well? But why target her like this? It felt really personal. And terribly unsettling.

'It wasn't like that,' she burst out in an urgent need to defend herself. 'It was obvious that Lara Chappel trusted him. She was with him willingly, anxious to make good her escape. Once we arrived at the airport, she thanked me very sincerely for my help. And I noticed she wasn't wearing any rings.'

It reminded Kathryn of the ring she was wearing herself—the ring proclaiming she'd agreed to marry Jeremy Haynes. Her gaze dropped to the flashy solitaire diamond he'd chosen for her and she told herself once again it was a measure of how much he valued her, not a status symbol of how much he was worth. Of course, money was useful. Life was a lot easier with it than without it. But sometimes...

She twisted the ring around on her finger, wishing it was an emerald, something more personal to her. Jeremy knew she loved green. Yet she couldn't very well argue against his romantic declaration that 'Diamonds are forever.' She heaved a rueful sigh and raised her gaze to the man who was stirring all sorts of troubling confusion in her.

He was staring at her ring, watching the agitated movement of it around her finger. She instantly stilled her hands and spoke very firmly. 'If a woman takes off her rings, it's a very deliberate action, meaning that relationship—her commitment to it—is over.

Lara Chappel wanted out of her marriage. I have no doubt of that. Ric wasn't abducting her. She looked at him as though he was performing a miracle for her.'

'A miracle...' Mitch Tyler's mouth twisted with irony as his gaze flicked up to meet hers. 'I see you're engaged to be married, Kathryn.'

'Yes.' Why did she feel defiant about that? He wasn't attacking her on it...was he?

'When is the happy wedding day?'

'We haven't decided yet.'

'No keen rush to the altar?'

She frowned, uneasy with these personal questions. 'It depends on work factors.'

'Your work or his?'

'I don't see how this is relevant to the situation that brought me here,' she flared at him.

'I assure you it is highly relevant,' he retorted, making a languid gesture that denied any attack. 'I'm simply ascertaining how long you want to remain in the position of Ric's executive assistant. Should your fiancé be happy for you to walk out of it today...'

'*I* wouldn't be happy,' she cut in emphatically.

'So you want to keep your job, regardless of any threat Gary Chappel might pose?'

She glared at him. 'You're supposed to take care of that.'

'Ah yes, the miracle worker,' he drawled. 'Ric plays knight to the rescue of his fair Lara, and I'm handed the job of slaying the dragon and keeping you safe.' His eyes beamed hard relentless purpose at her. 'And I will. I will keep you safe, Kathryn. But the

legal moves will take a day or two and I'm just wondering how much your fiancé cares about you and
your safety.' One eyebrow lifted in challenge. 'As
much as Ric, taking his woman right out of reach?'

'I'm not stupid. I can take care of myself,' she protested.

'Not against a man like Gary Chappel,' came the
flat retort. Then more softly, insidiously touching a
raw memory, 'How did you feel when he confronted
you in your office?'

She shuddered.

Mitch Tyler instantly pounced on the response.
'You were frightened.'

'He was in a rage.'

'Breathing fire. He not only has a lot of fire-power,
Kathryn, but he has no conscience about using it. If
Gary Chappel thinks you're standing in his way...'

The telephone rang. Mitch Tyler snatched up the
receiver and listened to the person on the other end
of the line.

It was a relief to have his attention withdrawn from
her, focused on something else. Kathryn reflected on
what he'd said about Gary Chappel, whom she'd
found a very scary man, having no regard whatsoever
for appropriate or even reasonable behaviour. She'd
managed to get rid of him once, but if he stormed
into the office again...or came to her home...

A man who had his wife watched and followed...a
battered wife...violence toward women...it was beginning to look very ugly to Kathryn. She remembered how he'd repeated her name, committing it to

memory for further reference, his contemptuous manner toward her, the sense of threat.

'Okay. So you've agreed to let Lara stay with you. That's fine but Ric can't stay, too.'

Mitch's curt words broke Kathryn's train of concern, alerting her to a new development.

'There have already been aggressive moves made by Gary Chappel to recover his wife,' he continued. 'I have Ric's executive assistant, Kathryn Ledger, here in my chambers, a protective move against further harassment in her office. In all fairness, Ric must become an open target for Chappel to pursue. Best if he flies out of the country as soon as possible—I mean tomorrow—get the heat off his Sydney office.'

Yes, Kathryn thought. She certainly didn't want another encounter with Gary Chappel.

A pause for listening, then, 'Get them both to call me when they arrive. I'll talk to Ric first but I also need ammunition from Lara Chappel to make legal moves stick. I have a plan of action in mind but it will only work with Lara's full co-operation.'

A plan of action… Kathryn breathed more easily. She instinctively had faith in Mitch Tyler's ability to counter-punch anything. If anyone had the power to take on a problem and beat it, he did. Ric had trusted him with it. She did, too. And now that communication with the escaping couple could be re-established, everything should be quickly settled.

Mitch put the receiver down. Kathryn tensed as his riveting gaze zeroed in on her again. 'Do you live with your fiancé?' he asked point-blank.

'Yes.'

'He'll be at home with you tonight?'

She shook her head. 'He's in Melbourne on business. He won't be home until tomorrow evening.'

'You can't be on your own, Kathryn. Not with Gary Chappel in a state of raging frustration. Believe me, I know what that man is capable of. Without some restraining force—and I can't even begin to apply that until tomorrow—he's a loose cannon.' He gestured to the phone. 'Want to call your fiancé? Ask him to fly back to Sydney this evening?'

While he was in the middle of negotiations for his future career in financial services? Calling him away from critical meetings to nurse-maid her? Because of something that had happened through her job? Which didn't matter as much as his, given that he'd be the main source of financial support when they had children.

'I don't want to do that,' she quickly decided. Jeremy would consider it totally unreasonable.

The blue eyes bored in. 'Aren't you more important to him than business?'

'I can take care of myself,' she asserted again.

'You're a woman…against a man with resources he'll have no compunction in using to get his own way.'

Jeremy would blame her for getting involved with something that was not really her job, bringing trouble upon herself, messing everything up for him. 'I can go to a hotel,' she said, desperately seeking an alternative course.

Mitch Tyler shook his head. 'If you won't call your

fiancé to come home and stand between you and any threat from Gary Chappel…you stay with me.'

Her heart skipped a beat. 'Stay…with you?' She could barely get the words out, her mouth had gone so dry.

'Ric made me responsible for you. I take that responsibility very seriously.'

'But…'

'I have a house in Woollahra. It has a guest suite which my sister and her husband use when they come to Sydney. You will be safe with me, Kathryn.'

He wouldn't allow anyone to get to her. She was sure of that. But safe with him? When he seemed to be driving stakes through her relationship with Jeremy with everything he said, everything he was?

I need to call Jeremy, she thought. *Stop this now.*

Yet she knew it would only cause an argument…in Mitch Tyler's hearing…and he'd be making silent judgements…stirring her up even more…making her wish…

No.

Better that she did stay with him. If she was so strongly attracted to this man, and the attraction remained strong throughout the evening, maybe she shouldn't be marrying Jeremy Haynes.

Kathryn looked down at the ring on her hand.

And the most troubling thing of all was…she wished she wasn't wearing it.

CHAPTER THREE

MITCH'S whole body was buzzing with adrenaline. He'd thrown down the challenge and every nerve was keyed to piano-wire tension, waiting for which way Kathryn would jump. Her gaze had dropped to the ring on her finger.

Take it off, Mitch fiercely willed. *If the guy won't drop everything to look after you at a time of need, he's not worthy of you.*

He was tempted to screw the challenge up another notch, offer to speak to the man himself, make him aware that Kathryn was in serious danger. But that might be tipping the scales which were delicately balanced at the moment. She was not stupid. He'd spelled out what the situation was. The ball was in her court. If she chose to stay with him…well, that choice would be very telling, indeed.

'I don't want to interfere with Jeremy's business,' she said slowly.

His heart kicked with excitement as she lifted her gaze to his, her eyes returning a challenge that demanded he measure up to his own promises.

'You claim I'll be safe with you…'

His groin tingled. It was definitely a sexual challenge. Did she feel the attraction, too? He cocked an eyebrow at her. 'Are you asking me if I'm a man of honour? If you can spend a night under my roof without my coming onto you?'

Heat whooshed into her cheeks, a sure sign that he'd hit a nerve that was pulsing with vulnerability. He smiled, wondering how tempted she was, though he spoke to dispel her unease.

'You're wearing a ring, Kathryn. You can count on my respecting it. Okay?'

The light mockery goaded her into accepting *safe* refuge with him. 'Okay,' she echoed on a long expulsion of obviously held breath. 'If you don't mind, I think it will be less fuss all around if I simply stay with you overnight.'

'Best if you remain in my house tomorrow, as well,' he pressed. 'Take a sick day from work. By tomorrow night there should be safeguards in place so you can resume your normal life.'

'All right,' she agreed, her beautiful green eyes glittering brightly above the scarlet cheeks.

He'd won, Mitch thought exultantly. She'd moved onto *his* ground. And she wasn't *married* yet. Her agreement could very well mean she was interested in finding out more about him, exploring the territory. Within limitations, Mitch forcefully reminded himself. The ring was still on her finger.

Still, his zest for life and all its challenges zoomed into overdrive. While he was waiting for Ric to call from Gundamurra, he took Kathryn through the scene Gary Chappel had made at the office, learning more about her and how she conducted herself in a crisis situation. Very cool and collected. Definitely not someone to be rolled over in a hurry. Yet she wasn't so cool with him, Mitch happily reflected.

Was her relationship with *Jeremy* rock-solid, or could he give it a shake? Was it her own pride insisting on not making *a fuss,* or couldn't she count on her fiancé to respond as he should? As much as Mitch wanted to believe the latter, it was clear that Kathryn Ledger was not a panic merchant and might simply be taking what she saw as a pragmatic course. Security was at hand in the person of Mitch Tyler. There was no need to bother her fiancé. The danger would be over by the time Jeremy walked back into her life.

All the same, Mitch couldn't help feeling elated that she had chosen to spend tonight with him. The thought struck him—*If I were her lover, I wouldn't like this choice one bit.* Yes, she was definitely playing with fire, and Mitch privately determined to stir the embers every which way he could, watching how the wind blew.

I'm playing with fire, Kathryn thought, feeling more and more unsettled by her decision to bypass Jeremy tonight and go with Mitch Tyler. It might have seemed a safe and sensible option but it wasn't. Somehow he was making her question where she was in her life and why, and the answers didn't feel so right anymore.

When the call came through from Ric Donato, diverting Mitch's attention from her, she told herself she could still change her mind. Yet as she sat listening to the one-sided conversation, she found herself totally captivated by his handling of the situation.

There was no criticism of Ric's actions. Mitch projected both sympathy and understanding for what had been done, and the strategy he outlined for involving Victor Chappel as a powerful restraining force on his son sounded good to Kathryn, as did the threat of negative publicity which would automatically accompany legal action if the restraint didn't hold.

She was particularly touched by the gentle tone he used when he rather hesitantly remarked, 'Patrick said…this is *your* Lara…from the old days.'

The old days… Kathryn wondered what the history was—how these men and Lara Chappel were connected, Ric Donato's enduring caring for her and their empathy for what he felt.

The conversation moved on to Kathryn's safety with Mitch, relating that her fiancé was away and she'd be spending the night with him. Ric asked to speak with her and she ended up promising him she'd do precisely what was planned. Too late to change her mind now. She felt caught up in a juggernaut of action that had to be followed.

Listening to Mitch elicit the information he needed from Lara Chappel was another fascinating experience—a sharp legal mind at work, yet the cross-examination was done sympathetically. Kathryn wasn't sure if this manner of his was simply clever or genuinely sincere, but she couldn't help being impressed by Mitch Tyler's sensitivity to others' feelings—his humanity in a field she would have thought was driven by ego.

On the other hand, she was sure he played to win. It was unimaginable that he wouldn't be a winner— the force of his energy overriding any opposition. If he was representing her in court, she'd have every confidence in his ability to gain whatever outcome was needed. But that was his professional life. What of his private one?

Clearly he couldn't be living with a woman or he wouldn't have offered her a room for the night in his home. He had a married sister and was obviously on good terms with her. No friction in his family as there was in Jeremy's where everyone was hitting off each other, intensely competitive.

She didn't like their habit of putting each other down. Winning meant too much to them. Though it certainly made them top performers in their fields, which was admirable. And as her mother had said, no doubt Jeremy would make a good provider as a husband.

He'd been very successful as a dealer in a merchant bank, drove a BMW Roadster, wore designer clothes, and his penthouse apartment at Pyrmont was very classy. If this next career step—becoming a partner in a very high profile financial services company— came off, he'd assured Kathryn they'd be set for life, riding high, nothing to worry about.

Except… Mitch Tyler had made her question how much Jeremy really cared about her. She'd justified his priorities in her mind, yet her heart felt oddly torn right now. Looking back over their relationship, hadn't she been the one to make all the adjustments, all the compromises?

She came from a caring family and it was natural to her to give what was needed, to create and maintain a happy atmosphere. But if something she needed clashed with Jeremy's ambition, his drive to be number one…would he drop everything to rescue her from a bad situation, as Ric Donato had done for Lara Chappel?

Here she was, staying with Mitch Tyler because she didn't want to put Jeremy to that test. Because… didn't she know in her heart he would fail it? Whereas all her instincts were telling her Mitch Tyler wouldn't. He was like Ric in that sense. Caring with passion. Caring that knew no limits. And Kathryn found herself fiercely wanting to be the object of such caring.

'Hungry?' Mitch shot at her from where he stood by the fax machine, waiting for Lara Chappel's written authorisation to act for her.

She glanced at her watch. Almost seven o'clock. Where had the time gone? 'I'm fine,' she said. 'What are we going to do about dinner?'

'I've got beef strips in the fridge, ready for a stir-fry. Won't take long to cook.'

'You cook?'

'Don't you?' he asked.

'Yes, but…obviously you work long hours. I thought…' He'd be like Jeremy, preferring to eat out. Though, of course, in these circumstances, going to a public restaurant was not a good idea. It wasn't as *safe* as having a private dinner…just the two of them…alone together.

Kathryn took a deep breath, trying to quell the uncomfortable sense of being disloyal to Jeremy. There was no denying Mitch Tyler was different but she shouldn't be comparing, shouldn't feel excited by the prospect of spending an evening with this incredibly mesmerising man.

'I like to cook,' he went on. 'It's relaxing. And I like to go home after a long day at work.' He threw a grin at her. 'Trust me. I'm a good cook. Though I'll let you help if you want to.'

'Okay.' She smiled back, quite charmed by the idea of preparing a meal together. A harmless activity, she decided. Nothing Jeremy could criticise.

The fax came through. Mitch filed it, then arranged for a courier to take the photograph with an accompanying request for a meeting to Victor Chappel. Satisfied that he'd set the ball rolling for a successful outcome, he called a taxi and by the time he and Kathryn emerged from his chambers, the car was waiting for them.

He held the passenger door open for her and waited until she was settled in her seat before getting in beside her. Sharing the suddenly enclosed space with him instantly set Kathryn's pulse racing. He was a big man with a heart-joltingly powerful presence, and far too attractive for her peace of mind. Feeling absurdly nervous about being with him, she fumbled with her seat belt, unable to fit it correctly into its locking slot.

'Let me,' he murmured, leaning over to help.

Rather than appear hopelessly inept she surrendered the task to him and instantly caught a whiff of some seductive male cologne as his face came closer to hers. She stared at his jawline, noting he had a five o'clock shadow and thinking he probably had hair on his chest, too. Would it be thick like the hair on his head, like his eyelashes?

'There. All fastened,' he said, the thick lashes lifting, his eyes locking onto hers, smiling eyes that simmered with warm pleasure in this simple act of looking after her, ensuring her safety.

Or was it more than that?

Her heart was galloping.

'Thank you.' She had to push out the words. They were barely a whisper.

'You're welcome,' he answered—a reply that anyone could have made. Yet somehow it seemed to encompass the sense that she was welcome in his life. He wanted her there. And it stirred in Kathryn a disturbingly strong desire to be there, too. Which she tried to dismiss as crazy. They'd only just met today. And she was committed to spending the rest of her life with Jeremy Haynes!

Mitch forced himself to settle back in his seat before he did the unforgiveable and kissed those very kissable lips. He'd given his word that she could trust him to act honourably, so any kind of sexual contact was out. Best not to touch her. Or even get too close. He had to keep temptation at bay, concentrate on mind games. Though he didn't want to play games with her, either. He wanted…to immerse himself in Kathryn Ledger and all that she was.

'What's your fiancé's name?' he asked, a streak of

jealousy provoking him into finding out more about his rival. 'Jeremy…?'

'Haynes.'

Mitch had never heard of him. 'Where do you live with him?'

'Pyrmont. An apartment overlooking the harbour.'

The guy had money then. Which was to be expected. Kathryn was quite a high flyer herself, running Ric's company in Sydney when he was overseas.

'Actually, the block of apartments does have security,' she added. 'You need a card to get into the elevator. If you just took me home…'

'No.' He flashed her a commanding look. 'Being alone is not a good idea.'

She was fiddling with her ring again, not looking at him.

Mitch cursed himself for reminding her of the man she planned to marry. 'I promised Ric I'd take care of you, Kathryn,' he quickly pressed.

She shook her head slightly, heaved a sigh, then ruefully conceded, 'And I promised him I'd go with you.'

'Is that such a hardship?' he half-mocked.

She grimaced. 'I'm sorry. I guess I sound ungracious. It's very kind of you to offer me the hospitality of your home.'

'It's not about kindness, Kathryn,' he whipped in, hating the remote politeness of her words.

'I know.' She flashed a wry glance at him. 'It would be easier if you were more…'

'More what? I'll try to oblige,' he promised, attempting to tease her out of her withdrawal.

'Older, fatherly, ugly, or just plain obnoxious,' she threw at him in an exasperated rush.

His heart danced with sheer joy. She was admitting an attraction. Beyond any doubt now. A wicked grin broke out. 'I can certainly be obnoxious if it will make you feel more comfortable.'

She laughed, a nervous little gurgle. 'I don't think play-acting will do it. In fact...' Her eyes were seriously curious. '...I'd like you to tell me about yourself. Your family. You mentioned a married sister.'

She wants to know me.

Normally Mitch didn't talk about his personal background. Who he was now—a barrister building a formidable reputation with every court appearance—seemed sufficient in itself for most people. If it wasn't, he simply declined to give out information that was none of their business. Yet it was different with Kathryn. He only had this one night to forge a bond that would hopefully overshadow whatever she had with her fiancé.

So he told her about Jenny, how she'd taken on the responsibility of caring for their disabled mother after their father had deserted them, how they'd managed on a social services pension, supplemented by handcrafts done by his mother and whatever Mitch could earn from a paper-boy run and cleaning cars—any jobs he could get after school hours. Tutoring had paid well, when he'd got older.

They'd been a tight-knit little family. Jenny had eventually trained as a nurse and married a doctor who currently had a practice at Gosford, on the Central Coast. Their mother had died of a stroke soon after the wedding, six years ago. Jenny now had a son and a daughter, both beautiful children.

He didn't mention the rape or the assault that had taken him to Gundamurra. That was deeply private, both to him and Jenny. Neither of them ever spoke of it. She'd moved past it, was happy in her life, and Mitch was content with that. Though he'd never forget it himself. One day he might tell Kathryn...if they ever reached that point of intimacy.

The taxi pulled up in front of his house. Woollahra was an old suburb of Sydney, fashionable now because of its proximity to the city centre, but most of the houses were of terrace construction, as they were in Surry Hills which had been considered almost a slum area with very cheap rentals in his boyhood. Though that had changed, too, for the same reason—close to the CBD, renovations upgrading the real estate.

He paid the fare, got out of the taxi and looked up at his home as he rounded the car to open the passenger door for Kathryn. It wasn't a classy apartment overlooking the harbour. It had no view at all, except onto this tree-lined street and the small courtyard at the back. But it satisfied something in him—perhaps a need to be rooted in something old and lasting.

He wondered what Kathryn would think of it.

He wondered what she thought of what he'd told her about his family background.

And he realised...for the first time in his life...he was feeling vulnerable. Not in any physical sense, but in his heart...where it mattered most.

CHAPTER FOUR

As MITCH ushered her toward his front gate, Kathryn looked up at the house, trying to distract herself from being so physically aware of him. Where he lived was another expression of the person he was and she could no longer deny she was interested in everything about him. But that was okay, she told herself, as long as sexual attraction didn't start blurring the line that should be kept.

This encounter was out of the ordinary.

Maybe her response to Mitch Tyler, the man, was being coloured by that.

His home was a two-storey terrace, painted a dark blue with white trim. Intricate white lace ironwork decorated the top balcony and lower porch. The street was certainly an upmarket one, every house neat and tidy, the trees along the sidewalk giving it a quietly contained atmosphere.

She knew that renovated terraces in this area were very pricey. Mitch Tyler had come a long way from being a paper boy. All on his own, too. No financial help from his family. Though, there'd certainly been a lot of love and care within that small household. A very impressive amount. *Good people,* her mother would say, warmly approving. Whereas Kathryn was very conscious of her parents' reticence on Jeremy's family.

Stop comparing, she berated herself, yet it was impossible not to, especially when Mitch showed her into his home and she instantly fell in love with it. The whole ground floor had been opened up for maximum living space yet the feeling of the place was still cosy, yet elegant, as well. No bombardment of fashionable colour and ultra-modern furniture.

The floors were a rich red-brown polished wood and the walls were all white, apart from the wonderful sandstone fireplace in the lounge room. Brown leather chesterfields flanked the fireplace and also the television set which was centred on the opposite wall and surrounded by bookshelves.

The dining room suite was a lovely mahogany with dark red upholstery, and scatter cushions on the chesterfields were of the same dark red which was repeated in woven borders on the cream floor rugs. On the coffee table sat a beautiful chess set carved from black and a creamy white onyx.

'Do you play?' she asked impulsively, wondering if it was purely a decorative item.

The blue eyes crinkled in amusement. 'It occupies what might otherwise be lonely hours. I play mostly correspondence chess, for lack of a handy partner.'

'I'll give you a game later,' she offered, seeing it as a safe activity to occupy the evening.

'You play?' He looked delighted.

'My father taught me—' she grinned '—for lack of a handy partner.'

He laughed. 'Do you play often?'

'Only when I go home alone. Jeremy doesn't...' She stopped before saying he didn't have the patience for chess, conscious of it sounding like a criticism, which wasn't fair. Jeremy worked very intensively. He liked more social activities in his leisure hours. Which was perfectly reasonable.

'You must tell me about your family while we deal with dinner,' Mitch smoothly invited, leading her to the kitchen which was the first part of an annexe built onto the back of the house. Laundry and downstairs bathroom beyond it, he told her.

The kitchen was white, too, apart from the red-brown granite benchtops—much more welcoming than the rather cold and clinical stainless steel everywhere, which Jeremy favoured because it was modern and the most expensive. Again Kathryn pushed aside the critical thought, telling herself that she should appreciate Jeremy's choice of state of the art kitchen fixtures. In fact, she should be grateful for them.

'Red wine okay with you? Or do you prefer white?' Mitch asked, shedding his suit coat and tie and rolling up his shirt-sleeves as he prepared to take charge of preparing their meal.

'Red, if we're having beef,' she replied before realising it might not be wise to drink any alcohol at all.

This was one occasion when she couldn't afford to let inhibitions slip, especially with Mitch's less formal appearance making her even more acutely aware of his sexy physique—taut cheeky butt, muscular arms, broad chest, an intriguing glimpse of black hair at the V end of his opened shirt. Still, one glass of wine shouldn't go to her head and there was no harm in being sociable to that small degree.

'If you want to go upstairs and freshen up while I

open this bottle and get organised, the guest suite is directly above this kitchen,' he tossed at her in casual invitation.

It was a considerate way of easing any tension about being shown to a bedroom and Kathryn instantly seized the opportunity for some respite from his overwhelmingly attractive qualities. She needed to get some proper perspective on this situation.

'Thank you. I won't be long.'

'Take your time. There's no hurry.'

The staircase was at the back of the dining room, the treads carpeted in teal-green, a floor covering which extended along the hallway above and into the bedroom she was to occupy. Kathryn was amazed to find the queen-size bed covered by an absolutely gorgeous woollen rug crocheted in multicoloured squares that were bordered by black. It was like a patchwork quilt, beautifully worked. And on the walls were framed tapestries patterned from famous paintings— the best of them, to her eye, a glorious water-lily scene, definitely one of Monet's.

This had to be some of his mother's handiwork, sitting in a wheelchair all day, keeping busy, selling what she could to specialty craft shops. Obviously not everything had been sold, or perhaps these lovely items had been worked after there had no longer been a need to sell. Kathryn liked Mitch Tyler all the more for keeping them, furnishing this room with them— the room his sister stayed in when she came to Sydney.

Family ties...

There was something very heart-tugging about this

room. Kathryn swiftly moved into the ensuite bathroom which was far more impersonal—mainly white with rows of teal feature tiles and towels. She looked at her face in the mirror above the vanity bench and wondered what Mitch Tyler saw in her. Was she the kind of woman who appealed to him? If she was free…would he…?

A rush of guilt stopped this treacherous train of thought. She was engaged to be married. Jeremy had been her partner for over a year. Their relationship wasn't perfect but whose was? It balanced out better than most, didn't it? To throw it all away on a chance meeting in extraordinary circumstances…

She lifted her left hand, stared down at the diamond ring on her third finger and once again found herself wishing it wasn't there. Did this mean that her commitment to Jeremy was wrong? Or was this just a passing feeling, a point in her life that was totally out of kilter with all the rest? If she took off the ring, it would signal to Mitch Tyler that…no! This was crazy. Far too fast. She would undoubtedly regret it tomorrow.

Besides, the evening with Mitch had barely begun.

This initial attraction could very quickly wear off.

Kathryn seemed more relaxed when she came back downstairs, happy to sit on the stool on the other side of the kitchen counter and cut up the vegetables he'd laid out for her. Mitch had worked swiftly while she was away, setting the dining table with place mats and cutlery, getting out the wok and various sauces, putting a pot of water on the stove, ready for the two-minute noodles to accompany the stir-fry. Now he could focus on drawing her out about herself and her family.

Though first she asked him if he'd designed the renovation of the terrace house himself. 'With the help of an architect,' he answered.

'And the decor is your choice, too?'

'Yes, it is,' he said a touch belligerently.

She nodded as though she'd guessed it was all his doing and he wondered what judgement she was making of it. Old-fashioned? Harriet had wanted to get rid of his mother's bedspread and tapestries—give them to his sister—but he wouldn't.

Too many hours of his mother's life were woven into them—hours shared chatting to him, caring about what he did, what he wanted to do. Good memories were worth more than stylish decor which invariably went in and out of fashion.

'That's a fabulous rug on the guestroom bed.'

He smiled, relieved by Kathryn's appreciation of it. 'My mother made it.'

'And the tapestries are her work, too?' she asked admiringly.

He nodded. 'She loved doing them.'

'I bet it gave her a lot of satisfaction, too. Like my mother with her pottery, creating something beautiful with her hands.'

It was a natural lead in to asking her about her family. She spoke of her parents with great fondness. Her father was a primary school principal, her mother an art teacher, and they lived at Gosford on the

Central Coast. Near where Jenny lived, Mitch thought.

'Dad is a born teacher,' she went on. 'He's really wasted in administration but he does run a good school so I guess that's a worthwhile achievement in itself, all the kids liking and respecting him.'

'A headmaster can make or break a school,' Mitch commented, remembering the one in his own boyhood, who'd never made a stand against bullying. 'I think a good one is worth his weight in gold to everyone under his care.'

Her face lit up with pleasure. 'I agree. Dad's had so many great letters from ex-pupils and parents. He's helped a lot of people.'

They chatted on amicably as the dinner was cooked, transferred onto plates and taken to the dining room. Mitch refilled their wineglasses. Kathryn seemed to hesitate over accepting more wine but let his action go, possibly deciding she didn't have to drink it.

It was interesting to learn that she'd trained as a graphic artist, moved into various promotional jobs, then gradually up the ladder to management, handling accounts in advertising before taking up her position with Ric. Clearly Ric trusted her decision-making, which said a lot about her, too.

Mitch was enjoying her company in every sense. He liked listening to her, watching her, and nothing hit a jarring note with him...except the diamond ring that said she belonged to another man. More and more he felt that had to be wrong. Or was he just too damned late on the scene to change what surely had to be a very serious decision on her part?

She was talking of her two younger brothers—one a pilot who loved flying, the other off back-packing overseas, discovering the world. Did *they* like the guy she'd chosen to marry? Were they confident she'd have a happy life with him?

Mitch wanted to ask these questions but knew they would sound too personal, too critical. Yet her lovely green eyes were dancing at him, sparkling with her own enjoyment in the comfortable rapport they'd established. How many people *clicked* like this?

His intense private reverie was abruptly broken by the sound of his front door opening. Alarm buzzed along his nerves, blowing his mind free of everything but danger signals. He was on his feet in a flash, body pumped with aggression, swinging to meet...

'Mitch...?'

Harriet! Calling out to him from the small vestibule which led into his lounge room. Harriet...using a key she should have returned! Mitch felt his jaw clench as he sensed Kathryn looking questions at him. Of all the people in the world, Harriet Lowell was the last person he wanted intruding on this far too short a time with a woman he really wanted.

Nor did his ex-lover have any right to enter his home uninvited!

The fear that had clutched Kathryn's heart as Mitch had erupted from his chair eased its panicky grip as she heard a woman's voice. It wasn't Gary Chappel breaking in, coming after her. It was someone with a key. A surprise visit from his sister?

Yet Mitch was still tense, and the emanation of violent anger from him was so strong, Kathryn felt herself almost cringing away from it. She tore her gaze from him to see who had stirred such a fiercely emotional response, and instantly felt a weird hollowness as the woman in question came breezing into the lounge room, wearing a slinky black wrap-around skirt with a halter top held together by thin straps, plus carrying a bottle of champagne and a large punnet of fresh strawberries.

'Mitch, darling—' brilliant white teeth smiled as her eyes lighted on him, smoking sexual promises '—quite a victory you had today. I thought a celebration was in order.'

She was tall and blond and beautiful, supremely confident of herself and her welcome in any company. Especially Mitch Tyler's since she had a key to his house. Kathryn wished there was a hole she could sink into.

'Then you thought wrong,' came the harshly cutting reply, jolting Kathryn into looking back at him. He was clearly furious, his jaw jutting out, black brows lowered. 'I'll see you out again, Harriet.'

Rather than being stunned into acquiescence, as Kathryn would have been, Harriet moved to meet him head-on, battle in her whole demeanour as her gaze zeroed in on Kathryn. 'So…you already have company. Where are your famed manners, Mitch?' she mocked. 'The least you can do is introduce us.'

She'd planted herself too far from the front door

for Mitch to force a retreat without manhandling her. He blocked any further progress into his house and presented an open palm to her as he curtly commanded, 'Give me the key, Harriet. You have no right to it anymore.'

'Oh, for God's sake!' she snapped. 'Can't you be civil?'

Pure ice answered her. 'I don't regard entering my home without permission civil.'

'Especially when you're embarking on a new affair,' she threw at him viciously. Her gaze targeted Kathryn again. 'I can't recall ever seeing you before. Definitely not from the upper echelons of legal circles.'

It was a snooty remark, ignored by Mitch. 'The key, Harriet,' he bored in with relentless purpose.

Her eyes poured scorn on him. 'You disappoint me, Mitch. I thought you were a competitor.'

'I choose the ring I stand in,' he stated bitingly. 'I won't be drawn into yours.'

'So you pick up the first bit of skirt you can find in retaliation?'

'Enough! I want you to go.'

'She won't measure up to me,' Harriet jeered.

'Your arrogance is totally ill-founded and this isn't winning you anything. In fact, you're turning into a very ugly loser. Please...give me my key and leave.'

'My hands are full with gifts for you.'

'Tools to get your own way,' he savagely corrected her, grabbing both the bottle and punnet from her hold, tucking the bottle in the crook of his arm so he could still extend his palm. 'Now your hands are free.'

She swung one back and Kathryn tensed, anticipating a violent slap. Mitch Tyler stood like an immovable rock, emanating a power that would certainly intimidate most people. She couldn't see his expression but Harriet had swift second thoughts about hitting him. She moved both her hands to the small shoulder-bag she wore, opening it to submit to his command which undoubtedly wasn't about to be retracted.

'No second chances with you, Mitch?' she commented bitterly.

'As you remarked earlier today, I have a black and white mentality.'

'You judge too harshly.'

'You chose a different bed, Harriet. Don't ever expect to come back to mine. There is no key that will give you entry to it.'

'You're going to regret this.' It sounded like a threat.

'Oh, I doubt it,' he drawled. 'Even if you sleep with all the judges on the bench, they still have to stick to the law.'

She slapped the key onto his palm. 'Going to give it to her now?' Her gaze snapped lofty contempt at Kathryn.

'Have some grace, Harriet. I wouldn't like my respect for you to slip even further.'

She glared at him but obviously found no crack in his armour to attack. Hating defeat, she haughtily turned her back on both of them and headed for the front door. Mitch followed, ensuring her exit from his home and making it secure against any further un-welcome intrusion.

Kathryn remained seated at the dining table, still absorbing the shock of what she had witnessed. No question that Harriet and Mitch Tyler had been lovers and her possession of a key indicated a high level of intimacy and trust, which had been broken, apparently by Harriet's sleeping with a judge.

A mistake she regretted?

A mistake Mitch wouldn't forgive.

An honourable man...dishonoured by infidelity.

And very, very angry about it.

Hurt.

Kathryn shook her head over her own foolishness in thinking the attraction she felt had been mutual. How could Mitch Tyler find her instantly desirable when she was so different in looks to the woman who'd been very recently sharing his bed? Nobody would describe Kathryn as beautiful. *Cute* was the word most frequently applied to her. And *cute* didn't cut it when a man like him could have a Harriet, who was obviously a barrister, too, sharing his world.

The violence of feeling this unheralded visit had stirred was proof enough that his emotions were still engaged with his sexy colleague, despite his decision to end their affair. It was ridiculous to have felt any danger in staying overnight in his home. The fault lay in herself, finding him so temptingly attractive. And that was wrong, too, when her emotions should also be engaged elsewhere. With Jeremy.

Kathryn twisted the ring on her finger, fiercely reminding herself that it promised fidelity—a promise she'd meant to keep. And *would* keep. Just as well Harriet had come, stopping her from possibly making a huge mistake. She should feel grateful to her, but she didn't. The pleasure in Mitch Tyler's company had all been taken away and she simply felt...hollow.

CHAPTER FIVE

IT GAVE Mitch no satisfaction to lock Harriet out of his home. The action was too similar to shutting the door after the horse had bolted. The damage was done. The rapport he'd established with Kathryn, the pleasant, relaxed mood...both were totally and irretrievably shattered by Harriet's arrogant presumption that she could seduce him into resuming their relationship.

Seeing Kathryn fiddling with her ring as he re-entered the lounge room telegraphed where her thoughts were—right back with Jeremy Haynes—and Mitch knew he had one hell of a battle on his hands to wrest back any ground he'd made with her. The caveman streak in him that had been tapped at their first meeting this afternoon, wanted to sweep her up and stamp himself back into her mind with a kiss that would knock his rival right out of it.

But she would fight him.

She would lose all trust in him.

It was a completely hopeless initiative that would damn him in her eyes and nullify any chance of moving forward with her. He knew this, yet it took enormous control to stop himself from taking some volatile action, to suppress the seething urge and force a reasonable response to what had just happened.

'I'm sorry you were trapped into witnessing what

you shouldn't have had to, Kathryn,' he said, trying to keep his intense frustration out of his voice.

She took a deep breath, squaring her shoulders as she turned her gaze to his. There was no warm vitality in her eyes—a dull flat green that left him in no doubt about her inner withdrawal. 'I shouldn't have been here,' she stated, her mouth twisting into an ironic grimace.

'You're here for a good reason,' he countered emphatically. 'And I might add I didn't introduce you to Harriet Lowell for the same reason. Better that she doesn't know your name, nor your connection to Gary Chappel.'

'Of course,' she muttered, nodding as though he'd just confirmed her place in his life—strictly business.

He wanted to yell that it wasn't so.

Heat flooded her cheeks. 'I'm sorry if I was in the way of...of some possible reconciliation.'

Words exploded from him in sheer vexation that she could imagine he might want Harriet back in his life. 'Kathryn, if you discovered your fiancé had cheated on you to gain some perceived advantage in his career, would you still want to be with him?'

Too much anger. He could see her gathering herself to answer him, forced into it.

'No, I wouldn't.' She lifted pained eyes, sympathetic eyes that made his guts writhe. He didn't want *sympathy* from her. 'I don't think cheating is ever justifiable,' she added quietly.

He didn't want her to *cheat* on Jeremy. He wanted her to *break* with him, but he saw little chance of that now.

'Case closed,' he said decisively. 'And may I add, your company is infinitely preferable to hers.'

This claim evoked a wry little smile. 'You've been very kind and hospitable.'

Her guard was up, well and truly, and Mitch didn't know how to reach past it. 'Kindness doesn't enter into it,' he stated flatly. 'Being with you is a pleasure.'

She shook her head. 'I've talked too much about myself. I guess…being a barrister…you're very good at drawing people out.'

'I wanted to know…just as you wanted to know about me, Kathryn,' he shot at her, fighting the barrier she'd obviously decided to raise.

'Yes. Well, it did pass the time and it's unlikely we'll ever meet again, so I don't suppose it matters what we say.' She pushed her chair back and stood up. 'We'd better clear the table now. Do the dishes.'

She was in full retreat.

The half glass of wine she'd left would not be drunk.

Mitch gathered up the glasses and condiments while she took the plates and cutlery. 'I'll make us some coffee,' he said as they headed for the kitchen. The need to prolong the evening with her was imperative. 'I'm looking forward to our game of chess,' he quickly added as she looked about to refuse coffee.

'Oh!' She frowned as though she'd forgotten her offer and now felt cornered by it.

'What do you like to play? Black or white?' he pressed.

Kathryn recalled what Mitch had said about chess occupying what would otherwise be lonely hours. If she retired to the guest suite now, she'd be leaving him to churn over the bitter scene with Harriet...alone with miserable memories. Hardly a kind return for looking after her, caring about her safety.

The embarrassment she felt was her own doing. Mitch Tyler had made every effort to put her at ease in his home and in his company. It would be mean to turn her back on him now. And there was nothing terribly personal about playing chess. They'd be concentrating on the game.

Black or white, he'd asked.

'Let's make it completely fair and toss for the choice,' she suggested.

'You *are* my guest,' he demurred, his face breaking into a grin of relief at her agreement to play.

'I don't want to be given any advantage.'

His eyes twinkled teasingly. 'Confident of winning anyway?'

Her chin tilted up with pride. 'I should warn you I was chess champion at school.'

He laughed. 'So was I.'

She looked askance at him as she rinsed their plates in the sink. 'Don't tell me you're a Grand Master.'

'Okay. I won't tell you.'

He was still grinning as he prepared the coffee-pot. Kathryn decided it didn't matter if he was far more skilled than herself. Playing was simply a means of keeping their minds distracted from other issues. He probably needed to win, given that he'd lost in love, though why on earth the beautiful Harriet had found anyone else more tempting...

Mitch had put it down to ambition.

Would Jeremy put ambition ahead of fidelity to her?

Being successful in his career meant a lot to him and he certainly had a hard, competitive streak, but Jeremy had given her no reason to believe he'd ever cheat on her. She'd been unsettling herself by questioning their relationship. Best to stop it right now.

Having washed and dried the plates and cutlery, she moved back to the stool on the other side of the kitchen counter while the coffee was brewing, putting some comfortable distance between herself and Mitch Tyler. It was difficult to ignore the sheer magnetism of his physical presence and silence made it even more nerve-tingling.

'Talking of winning, what was the victory you had today?' she blurted out, then instantly realised it was a tactless blunder, reminding him of Harriet's excuse for bringing champagne and strawberries to celebrate.

'The Barrington case.' He was preparing a tray with mugs and a plate of chocolate wafers and slanted her a sardonic look. 'If you could call squeezing a decent settlement out of a heart of stone a victory.'

Kathryn knew what he was talking about. The Barrington family dispute had been a rather scandalous case, widely reported in the media, the son having committed suicide, the daughter-in-law blaming the family and seeking compensation. 'I take it you were on the side of the underdog.'

He nodded. 'Harriet represented the family.'

'Oh!' Kathryn felt confused. Why would Harriet

want to celebrate *his* victory if...? 'She didn't mind losing?'

He gave a short derisive laugh. 'Harriet hates losing anything. Even me.'

Especially you, Kathryn thought. Obviously the beautiful barrister had been bending over backwards to regain some foothold in his life tonight. Which begged the question... 'I realise you feel responsible for me, because of Ric, but if I hadn't been here...'

'It would have made no difference.' The blue eyes stabbed that point home. 'Stop worrying about it, Kathryn.'

She wasn't sure about that. After all, he hadn't asked Harriet to give his key back until tonight. Why the oversight if he was dead against resuming any relationship with her? Barging right in as she had, might well have worked for her if Mitch hadn't been otherwise occupied with what was basically Ric Donato's business—emergency measures in response to his friend's plea for help.

As though he was tuned into her line of logic, he said, 'She knew damned well using that key was an invasion, but it's typical of her. Harriet is a risk-taker. I would have demanded its return before this, except—' his grimace carried distaste '—we've been on opposing sides in this court case. I didn't want to get into personal issues with Harriet when we were in professional conflict. Being a stickler about returning my key seemed inappropriate.'

His curt tone and the steely pride on his face told Kathryn to back off this sensitive ground. Stupid of her to pursue it in the first place. He had to be still hurting over it and here she was, turning the knife in the wound, just to satisfy her own curiosity about his feelings for another woman.

For what purpose?

It wasn't as though she wanted him for herself.

She had Jeremy.

The coffee was poured. Mitch carried the tray into the lounge room and Kathryn followed him, relieved they could now settle down and play chess without any need to make conversation. The silence would be natural, not awkward or tense. She could focus on the game. Relax. Stop questioning what should be...was... beyond questioning.

Mitch couldn't concentrate on chess. He felt totally hamstrung by the situation. He pondered telling Kathryn straight out that meeting her had told him unequivocally that his previous relationship with Harriet Lowell had lacked the more instinctive attraction he felt with her, had even lacked the power to stir him anywhere near as strongly as she did. Could he lay himself on the line that far? Would it hit a chord with Kathryn, or would it embarrass her?

His hands moved the chess pieces in automatic defensive moves to her attack. Before he even saw it coming she had him checkmated. 'I've been blindsided,' he muttered in self-deprecation as he conceded the game.

Her eyes twinkled both pleasure in the victory and challenge because it was too easy. 'I think you underestimated me.'

'I won't a second time,' he warned, his heart lifting

as he felt the connection again. She had to feel it, too. It couldn't be one-sided.

But her lashes swept down as she set up the chess pieces for another game, clearly determined on blocking out anything of a personal nature. 'Would you like to play white this time?' she asked, intent on being fair.

'No. I'm fine with black. I like to come from behind.'

Her gaze lifted in a flash of amusement. 'Making victory all the sweeter?'

'I wish,' he said with feeling.

For one poignant moment she smiled full on and his heart leapt with triumphant pleasure at the instant tug of what had to be mutual attraction—strongly positive. Yet it was far too fleeting to make any capital out of it. The next instant she was staring at the chessboard again, selecting a pawn to move forward, and the shut-out was warning enough not to push for anything beyond her current comfort zone.

He forced himself to focus on the game. He didn't win. He didn't lose, either. They reached stalemate and both of them conceded a draw. He insisted on a third game, just to keep her with him, though he knew it wouldn't change anything. Loyalty—fidelity—to her fiancé was firmly entrenched in her mind.

He won this time and she used his victory as an excuse to retire with equal honours, saying she was tired and thanking him for playing with her.

'We're a good match,' he couldn't resist saying.

'I enjoyed it,' she acknowledged, then rather nervously rushed on, 'About tomorrow, Mitch...'

'I'll be gone early in the morning,' he broke in, knowing she would avoid having breakfast with him, seeing him off. 'Just make yourself at home here. I'll call and let you know the outcome of my meeting with the Chappels.'

'If it's positive, I could go back to work, pick up my car…' She was anxious to be away from him and the intimacy of his home.

'No!' he cut in emphatically. 'Better not to be too confident and hasty, Kathryn. When do you expect your fiancé home?'

She frowned. 'About six-thirty tomorrow evening.'

'I'll feel happier delivering you safely to him myself.' And checking out what he was like. Mitch couldn't bring himself to let Kathryn Ledger go without satisfying himself it was right to do so. Right for her. It was never going to feel right to him.

'Surely that won't be necessary,' she argued, not liking that scenario.

If it made trouble with her fiancé, good! Mitch thought savagely. 'He should be told what's gone on, Kathryn. I'm not sure I can stop Gary Chappel from making a dangerous nuisance of himself outside your business hours. Especially where there are no witnesses. Your fiancé will have to be your watchdog and protector.'

She heaved a fretful sigh. 'All right. But I don't need you to tell him, Mitch. I can do that myself.'

'Okay.' They were fighting words and he had no authority over her life to override them. 'Just let me take you home and pass you over to him. That way

I can assure Ric I let no harm come to you. Fair enough?'

The reminder of her work situation with Ric had to have impact on her resistance to his plan. Her boss had made her promise to go along with Mitch's advice and Mitch would report back to Ric. Besides, if her relationship with Jeremy Haynes was all it should be, there was no reason for her not to accept Mitch's escort home.

Her reluctance smacked of conflict.

Which gave Mitch a flicker of hope that she might change her mind about this marriage. Unlikely, he warned himself, yet the desire to have her for himself—at least explore what was possible between them—would not lie down and die.

'I'm sorry if I sound ungrateful...difficult...' She grimaced in apology. 'I guess I'm not used to any need for protection.'

'The need is real,' he gravely assured her. 'Don't dismiss it, Kathryn. In my opinion, Gary Chappel is psychopathic.'

She shuddered, possibly in memory of Chappel's behaviour at her office. 'Okay. I'll wait for you to take me home,' she conceded in a rush.

'The best course,' he said approvingly.

She managed a wry little smile. 'Thanks for looking after me, Mitch. Good night.'

She was off, walking away from him, and all Mitch had from her was a toehold on tomorrow.

It was not a winning position.

But he would not accept defeat until it was staring

him in the face. All these years he'd never met a woman who made him feel as Kathryn did.

Ironic that it should happen on the very day Ric had taken charge of Lara's life. Eighteen years...and still Ric cared about her. A one-woman man.

Might Kathryn Ledger be *his* one-in-a-lifetime woman?

Maybe it was just the wrong time for them. Ric and Lara had been separated. She'd married someone else. They'd connected again now. Lara had taken off her rings to go with Ric.

Kathryn had to take off that damned ring.

Until she did...there was no future for them.

There might never be a future for them.

Ships passing in the night...

Everything within Mitch revolted against that concept.

Somewhere there had to be a twist that worked his way.

CHAPTER SIX

KATHRYN was grimly reciting, *Please be home. Please be home. Please be home...* all the way up in the elevator to Jeremy's apartment. She'd deliberately cut her time with Mitch Tyler as short as she could, getting Jeremy to call her once he'd got into a taxi at Mascot Airport so she didn't have to wait until he was actually in residence before Mitch drove her from Woollahra to Pyrmont.

She'd been tense in the car, still disturbed by the powerful attraction of Ric's friend, feeling almost desperate to be distanced from it, get her life back into its normal flow. Here in the elevator, her nerves were literally twitching with dreadful agitation at the thought of being forced to invite Mitch in to wait for her fiancé's arrival. She didn't want any shadow of his presence left behind in the apartment she shared with Jeremy. Bad enough that the two men were going to come face-to-face, making more comparisons inevitable.

At last the elevator halted and opened onto the penthouse floor. She had her key out ready. Just a few more seconds and she could say goodbye to the man accompanying her every step. She pressed the buzzer to alert Jeremy to her arrival then shoved the key in the lock, hoping he would come to the door as it was opened so Mitch would be satisfied about her safety and go. Then she'd be able to relax with everything that was familiar to her instead of feeling hopelessly messed around.

To her immense relief, Jeremy was as eager to see her as she was to see him. As she swung the door wide, he was striding across the penthouse foyer, his handsome face beaming with happy anticipation. He stretched out his arms to wrap her in an exuberant embrace and she rushed in to be wrapped, wanting the comfort of feeling herself loved by him.

'Hey! Have I got news for you, babe!' he crowed triumphantly, hugging her tightly, even swinging her off her feet.

'Um…just a minute, Jeremy. There's someone with me,' she babbled breathlessly.

'Who?' He looked over her head in careless good humour and Kathryn strained against his hold to make one last acknowledgement of Mitch, who was now standing in the doorway, watching her reunion with her fiancé, the blue eyes coolly assessing, his strong face grimly etched.

She had to swallow hard before she got out the words, 'This is…'

'It's okay, Kathryn,' he cut in, apparently not wanting an introduction. 'I can see I'm not needed. I'm off.'

He raised one hand in a brief salute, while using the other to grab the door and close it, making his departure both abrupt and decisive, not even waiting for her to thank him again.

Quick and clean, which was what she'd wanted, Kathryn fiercely told herself, yet that strange hollow feeling attacked her again…like something vital had been ripped out of her.

'Who was that guy?' Jeremy demanded, curiosity piqued enough to forget his own excitement for a moment.

'My protector,' she said wryly.

'What?'

'It's a long story.' Time to concentrate on Jeremy now. She'd left text messages on his mobile phone but apart from the one airport call she'd requested, they hadn't spoken—no communication about his meetings in Melbourne nor the disruption at her own office. She hung her arms around his neck again, telling herself *this* was the man she loved and stretching her mouth into a big welcoming smile. 'I want to hear your news first.'

He was bursting with it. So much so, he didn't even kiss her. His grin was far too wide for puckering up. 'I got the partnership.' His eyes sparkled with delight in the achievement—bright brown eyes, much warmer than blue. 'I'll be heading up the Sydney branch with two other guys, starting next week.'

'But won't you have to work out your notice at the bank?' They surely wouldn't want to lose such a high-powered and immensely successful dealer so quickly.

'Not in my position,' Jeremy declared with supreme confidence. 'They can't risk my tapping clients from them. Once I tell them I'm leaving, I walk the same day. And that day will be tomorrow.'

'Wow! That's really moving,' she commented appreciatively.

'Up and up. With you at my side, babe.' He tucked her appropriately at his side, an arm curled around her shoulders, walking her into the living room and waving to the bottle of champagne he'd set on the kitchen counter. 'I had the taxi stop at a liquor store. Celebration is definitely in order.'

No strawberries, she thought, and mentally kicked herself for equating Jeremy's victory with Harriet Lowell's visit to Mitch Tyler's home last night.

'You open the bottle. I'll get the glasses,' she offered eagerly, needing some pleasant bubbles in her head. 'And tell me all about your meetings from start to finish.'

Jeremy was only too happy to give her a blow-by-blow description. Kathryn moved into the stainless-steel kitchen while he popped the cork. She placed his prized crystal flute glasses ready for him to do his skilful pouring, then quickly asked, 'What do you want to do for dinner?'

'Oh, just get a couple of pizzas out of the freezer,' he said with a dismissive wave.

Clearly food wasn't important tonight and he wanted her complete attention, no distraction with cooking. Which she always did when cooking was called for. Jeremy was never going to share that with her. It wasn't in his nature to even think of it or want to do so.

On the other hand, on a great provider scale, he was definitely a ten, so she had nothing to complain about. Just because Mitch Tyler...no, she wasn't going to think about how...*companionable*...it had been with him—sharing the preparation of their meal last night.

She took the pizzas out of the freezer, stripped off their covering, switched on the oven, slid them in, picked up her glass of champagne and focused fully on the man she'd chosen as her future husband. He was glowing; smile, skin, eyes. Clean-cut good looks that any woman would admire, especially when he was full of zappy energy, as he was at the moment, recounting how he'd gone about impressing the other partners in the financial services company he'd targeted.

He wore his dark brown hair in a rather yuppie style, short at the sides, long enough at the top for a natural wave to soften his high forehead and complement the rather acutely angled arch of his eyebrows. Very attractive. Striking. And while his physique was on the slender side, it enabled him to wear fashionable clothes well, which he did with considerable panache. Kathryn had always felt proud to have him as her partner.

And not just for presentation, either. He was very smart, right on the ball with clever and amusing repartee, and she admired his drive to be the best at what he did. Most women would say she'd hit the jackpot with Jeremy Haynes, and she had. Of course, she had.

So why didn't she want to make love with him tonight? Why was she glad he hadn't kissed her in the foyer, with Mitch Tyler watching? Why was she looking at his mouth and thinking of another man's? She should be listening to him with avid ears. This was their future he was talking about. A shining future that would support any family they chose to have.

He described the subtle manoeuvres he'd used, how he'd pressed all the right buttons to win over this person and that person, the top-class Melbourne restaurants where he'd been breakfasted, lunched, wined and dined while all the power-brokering had been done.

Quite a comedown having heated up pizza, Kathryn thought as she took them from the oven and sliced them up for easy eating. Still, the Krug champagne certainly upgraded the meal and fuzzed the tensions she'd brought home with her. She encouraged Jeremy to refill her glass, having downed the first faster than she usually would. There was no need to keep her guard up tonight. In fact, there was every need to start feeling some sexual desire where it should be directed.

They moved to the glass dining table which was supported by two blocks of shiny black granite. The black lacquered chairs were some kind of moulded plastic, the seats and backrests curved for comfort but they were hard and cold to sit on. The design was very modern, of course.

They finished the pizza and were still swilling their champagne when Jeremy finally ran out of steam over his doings and asked about hers. 'So tell me who was the guy at the door, and why did he think you needed protection?' he tossed out in a lightly mocking tone, suggesting he couldn't believe the situation to be a serious one. Or if it had been, it was over and done with, hardly worth mentioning.

Kathryn was niggled by his attitude. It reinforced her feeling that his career was far more important than her safety, and okay…she'd put it first, too, but was that right? Goaded by a sense of her own worth, she started with the status of *her protector*.

'You know the Barrington court case that's been news headlines lately.'

He nodded. 'Heard it was settled yesterday.'

'Well, the man who accompanied me home is Mitch Tyler, the barrister who settled it for the daughter-in-law.'

That raised Jeremy's eyebrows. 'What was he doing with you?'

'Making sure I wasn't accosted by Gary Chappel of the nursing home Chappel family.'

He looked stunned by this news. The shock was swiftly followed by alarm. 'Why would Gary Chappel want to accost you?'

His alarm lifted a considerable weight from Kathryn's heart. Jeremy really did care about her safety.

She proceeded to tell him about the photograph that had turned up on the computer this morning, her boss's reaction to it, his subsequent action in going to Vaucluse and masterminding Lara Chappel's escape from her situation, her own part in evading the pursuit vehicle and driving them to Bankstown Airport.

Jeremy looked aghast as she recounted what she had done to help. 'Ric Donato involved you in this madness?'

She frowned. 'I don't consider it madness to rescue a battered wife, Jeremy.'

'A black eye is not necessarily a battered wife,' he argued.

'Well, it is to me,' she retorted hotly. 'And it wasn't only that. He was having her watched, followed…'

'Maybe for good reason,' Jeremy shot back at her. 'What if she was cheating on him?'

'She was frightened of him, Jeremy. And grateful to Ric for…'

'This is *Gary Chappel's* wife we're talking about,' he almost shouted, then rose from the table in obvious agitation, pacing around, too disturbed to remain seated. 'Does *he* know about your part in this?'

'Not about driving them to the airport. But he did come into the office after they'd gone, demanding to know where they were.'

'And you didn't tell him?'

Kathryn paused to take a deep breath, feeling shaken and confused by Jeremy's reaction which was terribly off-key to her. 'No. I didn't tell him. I wanted Ric and Lara to get safely away. And let me tell you, he's a very scary man,' she added more strongly.

'It's only natural he'd be angry,' Jeremy instantly excused.

'It wasn't just anger. It was…' How to describe the sense of vicious and malevolent threat? 'Mitch Tyler says Gary Chappel is a psychopath and I believe him,' she blurted out.

'Right!' Jeremy snapped. 'So it comes down to you having to be protected from *him.*' He glared furiously at her as he added, 'From the man who's going to be my biggest client when I start my new job next week. I'll be his financial adviser, Kathryn. In charge of the Chappel millions, if not billions. He is a *huge part* of our future.'

She stared at him, seeing how very much he cared about this connection, realising it came ahead of anything else. Jeremy would deal with the devil if there was a big enough reward in it. A chill started in her bones and seeped through her, raising goose bumps on her skin.

'I presume he got your name while you were *blocking* his pursuit of his wife,' he ran on. 'And the fact you're Ric Donato's executive assistant.'

'Yes, he did,' she answered flatly.

'My fiancée.' He threw up his hands as though she'd committed the worst possible evil. 'That's great. That's just great!'

'The solution is perfectly simple, Jeremy,' she heard herself say. 'I can stop being your fiancée.'

'Oh, don't be ridiculous!' he tossed at her, his eyes glittering with the need to find a different option. 'First off, you'll have to leave that job, distance yourself from Ric Donato instantly.'

Her jaw started clenching. 'I won't do that.'

He sliced a dismissive gesture. 'You don't need it. Once I start working as a partner in this business, we'll be on easy street for life. You can be a lady of leisure.'

'I like my work, Jeremy. And I won't walk out on Ric when he has to be somewhere else.'

His furious pacing jerked to a halt as an idea struck him. '*Where* is the somewhere else?'

'I don't know yet. Mitch Tyler advised him to get out of the country as soon as possible. Ric said he'd contact me about his destination before he flew off.'

'*With* Lara Chappel?'

He'd seized on that so fast, Kathryn paused, her instincts warning her she shouldn't give Jeremy this information. He'd use it. He'd use it to somehow further his connection with Gary Chappel, work it to get some advantage.

'I don't know,' she replied, watching him from what felt like a long distance. A very cold distance.

'Where are they now?' he demanded.

'I don't know that, either.'

'You drove them to Bankstown Airport,' he bored in.

'And left them there. I had to get back to the office.' She was glad now she hadn't mentioned Johnny Ellis's private plane. Bad enough that she'd given out the airport clue.

'But Ric must have told you what he had planned.'

'No, he didn't. He said the less I knew, the better. And he trusted me to cover his tracks, Jeremy,' she said very pointedly.

'What Ric Donato wants isn't important,' he stated with breathtaking arrogance.

'It is to me,' she bit out.

Again her feelings and her position were summarily dismissed. 'We give Gary Chappel the information he wants. All we can get that will help him.' He actually grinned as he added, 'In fact, that's the best protection for you, Kathryn. He certainly won't think of harming you under those circumstances.'

Loyalty to her employer didn't matter.

Giving Lara up to an abusive husband didn't matter, either.

This man—the man she had planned to marry—had no sense of morality.

None at all.

Money was his God and he'd serve it, regardless of who got hurt.

His eyes narrowed. 'Best that you do keep working for Ric. Gives you the inside track on what moves he makes.'

'Better still if I'm not your fiancée, Jeremy,' she said with icy precision. 'Then you have no connection to anyone involved in Lara Chappel's escape from her rotten husband. You're free and clear of it.'

'No...no...we can use this to our advantage.'

'Your advantage. Not mine. And I won't be a party to your plan which I find absolutely obscene.'

'Kathryn—' He felt vexed impatience with her attitude '—you don't understand how power works.'

Oh, yes, she did. There was power for evil and power for good and Jeremy and Mitch Tyler were at opposite poles of it. Black and white.

She took off the flashy diamond ring, set it on the glass table, rose from the shiny black chair, looked Jeremy straight in the eye and without the slightest hesitation, declared, 'Our engagement is over. I don't want to be attached to you anymore, Jeremy. And believe me, you'll be better off not mentioning any of this to Gary Chappel. You might end up biting off more than even you can comfortably chew.'

CHAPTER SEVEN

Three months later...

IT WAS four-thirty in the afternoon when the case for the prosecution rested. Court was adjourned, allowing the defence to start fresh in the morning. Mitch accompanied his client out, assuring him everything was prepared for tomorrow. His clerk handed him a message and instantly warning bells rang in Mitch's mind.

The message read—'Call Patrick as soon as possible.'

Gundamurra...

Only two nights ago, Ric had telephoned him, wanting advice on returning to Australia, to Lara, and whether Gary Chappel was still a threat?

He'd sounded very stressed.

Had he done something stupid?

Mitch had warned him there was no absolute assurance that Gary was out of the picture. To his mind, a psychopath never dealt straight, even while giving every appearance of it. He also cautioned Ric that Lara might need more time to recover from the ordeal of her marriage.

After Jenny's one traumatic experience, she had shied away from men for years. He knew from the information Lara had given him to sue for divorce that she had suffered much more abuse than a single rape. She would be grateful to Ric for rescuing her but accepting love from him…even being with him might cause her painful conflict.

These thoughts raced through his mind as he took off his barrister's wig and gown, handed them to his clerk and took out his mobile phone. It wasn't Patrick but his housekeeper, Evelyn, who answered his return call.

'I can't fetch Mr Patrick right now. He's with Miss Lara. But he told me to tell you what happened here. A plane crashed on our airstrip about an hour ago. It shouldn't have tried to land. It's all mud here from the big wet. Only a helicopter can come in. Anyway, the pilot didn't radio to find out, just brought it down. The plane was a charter from Sydney and Miss Lara's husband was on it. Gary Chappel. He died in the crash. Mr Patrick thought you should tell Mr Ric. Okay?'

Gary Chappel at Gundamurra…dead!

Mitch gave himself a quick mental shake. 'Okay. Thanks, Evelyn. I'll contact Ric and let him know.'

Except he didn't know where Ric was—London? New York? Los Angeles? He hadn't queried where Ric was calling from when they'd spoken two nights ago.

Another shock hit him. Ric had mentioned Gundamurra in that conversation and Gary Chappel had turned up there today. Was there a connection? Could his home telephone be bugged? He'd have to get someone in to check it out, sweep the whole house for any surveillance gadgets. It appalled him to think that Gary Chappel might have got to Lara through…

But it didn't matter now. The man was dead. Good riddance, too. Lara was free of him forever now. And Ric could come home without endangering either her or himself. Or Kathryn.

Kathryn…

She would know where Ric was.

He glanced at his watch. She should still be at her office. He could call her… No, dammit! This was as good an excuse as any to go and see her. Why not? It gave him the opportunity to check that Jeremy Haynes was still very much the man in her life.

He called Ric's business number, ascertained from the receptionist that Kathryn was still at work in her office, and asked for a message to be relayed that Mitch Tyler was on his way with urgent business and would she please wait for him to arrive.

As he put away his mobile and headed out of the courthouse to catch a taxi, he smiled grimly over the tactic to force one more encounter with Kathryn Ledger. Probably another exercise in frustration. He remembered only too well how she had rushed into her fiancé's arms when he'd escorted her to the Pyrmont apartment.

A penthouse apartment.

Hard to beat a guy who not only looked like a million dollars but undoubtedly had millions of dollars, as well. Still, the same description could have been applied to Gary Chappel. Money wasn't everything. The problem was…Mitch had no reason to think Jeremy Haynes wasn't treating Kathryn right, looking after her.

He'd instructed her to contact him immediately if there was even a whiff of trouble from Gary Chappel.

She hadn't called.

The message he'd just sent would probably alarm her but he could straighten that out soon enough. And seeing her again might even help him get over the gnawing sense of having missed out on something too good to be missed. Three months...had he been exaggerating the memory of how he'd felt with her?

He flagged down a passing taxi, gave the address at Circular Quay to the driver, and settled back in the passenger seat for the short drive to his destination. Ever since meeting Kathryn Ledger, he hadn't felt a spark of interest in any other woman. Harriet certainly left him cold. He could barely bring himself to be civil to her when they met professionally. Ironic that she'd tried to dig out the identity of 'the mystery woman' in his life, getting no satisfaction because Kathryn was not *his woman*, much as he would have liked her to be.

He wondered if Ric would have any luck with Lara, now that Gary Chappel was gone. Best to get his mind focused on the urgent business before he walked in on Kathryn. No point in nursing any hope that she'd suddenly have a change of heart over marrying Jeremy Haynes. He just wanted to see her...

Kathryn's heart wouldn't stop fluttering. Mitch Tyler, coming to her on urgent business! It had to be something to do with Gary Chappel. Or Ric. Possibly both of them.

There'd been a business e-mail from Ric waiting for her in her office computer this morning. No suggestion of trouble. But that had been sent last night. Now was now, and Mitch was coming in person, which had to mean it was a weighty matter, not something he would tell her over the phone.

Ric had been more or less on the run for the past three months, visiting his overseas offices, but as far as she knew, his safety hadn't been threatened. Neither had her own. Gary Chappel had not accosted her again in this office, nor anywhere away from it.

Jeremy had obviously remained quiet about his past association with her, probably deciding it *was* wiser to have no personal link to Lara Chappel's disappearance. Certainly he'd not tried any contact with her since she'd moved into the small Bondi Junction apartment she now called home. So much for all his professions of love! He'd told her point-blank that *she* was making the mistake in breaking up with him.

A big, stupid mistake.

Maybe he'd thought she'd come grovelling back to him.

Not in a million years!

In any event, her move had not put her in any danger. As far as she was aware, no-one had been following her or checking up on her. No confrontation. No threat. Nothing.

But maybe these past three months had been the lull before the storm—assuring Victor Chappel that the line was being toed, so if anything happened to Ric now…

She was pacing around her office, her mind in a whirl of worry when Mitch Tyler was shown in by her secretary. The sheer physical magnetism of the man instantly scattered her wits. Needles of awareness attacked her body. She stood still, trying to absorb the impact of meeting him again. Her fogged mind did register the fact that he was taking stock of her, too, not rushing into a greeting.

He was scanning her from head to toe, as though matching her to the imprint in his memory. She could feel her blood heating in response to the trail his gaze took. It was totally embarrassing to realise she was reacting sexually, her breasts tightening, her stomach contracting, her thighs going weak.

She desperately tried reminding herself of Harriet Lowell, the kind of woman he found attractive, but it didn't lessen her own response to him one bit. She felt caught up in a dynamic force that drained her of any resistance to the attraction tugging at her. It took an act of will to get her mouth working.

'Mitch…?'

'Kathryn…' He spoke her name on an expulsion of breath that seemed to fan the heat inside her.

'Is there trouble?' she asked, virtually jerking the words out.

'No trouble,' he assured her. 'I've just had word that Gary Chappel died in a plane crash this afternoon.'

'Died…?' The shock of this news served to get her thoughts off Mitch Tyler and her reaction to him.

'Where did it happen? Was it a big plane? Many casualties?'

'No. Small plane. Private charter. As far as I know, he was the only casualty. And probably his fault, not wanting the pilot to radio ahead to Gundamurra to inquire if the airstrip was fit for landing.'

'Gundamurra?' She'd never heard of the place.

'It's an outback sheep station. Where Ric took Lara, Kathryn.'

The outback!

How on earth did Ric know a safe refuge in the outback?

But that wasn't the point.

'Gary Chappel found out?' Her mind instantly spun to Jeremy. Had he told *his client* about Ric's flight from Bankstown Airport? Had Johnny Ellis's plane somehow been traced to its destination?

Mitch grimaced. 'I suspect an illegal tap on my home telephone. But that's irrelevant now.'

Irrelevant...yes, thank God! A surge of relief swept aside the awful sense that she might be responsible, betraying Ric's confidence to a man she'd thought she could trust with it.

'I thought you'd know where Ric is now,' Mitch went on. 'He'd want to know immediately. He's been moving around so much...'

'London. He e-mailed me from his London office last night.' She checked her watch, mentally calculating the time difference. 'Right now he should be asleep in his apartment at Knightsbridge. I have that number. I'll call it for you.'

She moved quickly around her desk, picked up the

telephone receiver, flicked open her teledex and proceeded to press the long string of numbers for the international call.

Mitch had walked forward to take the receiver once contact was made. He stood on the other side of her desk, waiting, his gaze dropping to the hand tapping out the numbers.

No diamond ring on her third finger!

He sucked in a quick breath as hope rocketed through him, kicking his heart into a faster beat, blowing all thoughts of Ric out of his mind. Kathryn was free! Unattached!

Or was she? The ring might only have been taken off temporarily for some reason…leaving it accidentally in the washroom, having it cleaned, fixed by a jeweler…

'It's ringing,' she said, holding out the receiver.

So were his ears—ringing with the wild thump of his heart. Ric's voice on the other end of the line demanded his attention. Somehow Mitch managed to impart the critical information in a coherent manner, but the perimeter of his mind was whirling around how best to ascertain the status of Kathryn's engagement to Jeremy Haynes.

Nothing had changed for him. Kathryn Ledger still hit deep basic instincts that no other woman had even twanged before. One look and she'd floored him again. If there was any chance…

Kathryn listened to Mitch's side of the conversation, imagining how relieved her boss would be to know there was no longer any threat to Lara or himself.

No need to wait for a divorce, either.

He could come home and be with the woman he'd risked so much for, a woman he cared about beyond any cost to himself. Kathryn ruefully wondered how it would feel if a man cared for her like that.

Jeremy certainly hadn't.

But Mitch Tyler...no, what good would it do her to fit him into that frame, stirring herself into wishing for a chance with him? Bad enough that she was so susceptible to his exceptionally strong charisma. At least she wasn't feeling quite so shaken by it now and should be able to deal courteously with his departure.

The call ended. The receiver was put down. 'Ric will be on the first flight he can get from London to Sydney,' Mitch informed her. 'No doubt you'll hear from him when he arrives.'

It forced her to meet his gaze directly. The blue eyes were so piercing, she felt hopelessly rattled again. 'Yes,' she said inanely.

'You're not wearing your engagement ring.'

The words were shot at her so fast and hard, her reply tumbled out in a defensive rush. 'I changed my mind about marrying Jeremy.'

'What changed it?' he bored in.

There were so many reasons, yet the only one she could acknowledge to Mitch Tyler without totally embarrassing herself centred on loyalty. 'Jeremy is a partner in a financial services company and Gary Chappel is...was...his client. He wanted me to... to...'

'Betray Ric?'

'Yes. To actually help Gary Chappel find his wife.'

'Gaining an advantage for himself,' came the cynical comment.

'I didn't realise he would trade integrity for ambition. I couldn't live with it.'

'That must have been one hell of a disillusionment, Kathryn.'

She grimaced. 'Better that I found out.'

'True.'

His forceful agreement reminded Kathryn of Mitch's *disillusionment*—Harriet bedding a judge to gain an advantage. It was on the tip of her tongue to make some quip about both of them suffering the same letdown from their partners, until she remembered three months had gone by. For all she knew, Mitch had patched up his relationship with the beautiful barrister. One infidelity wasn't quite the same thing as selling integrity for money.

She heaved a sigh to loosen the tightness in her chest and ruefully remarked, 'You must be very effective at cross-examining people in court, Mitch. I haven't even told my parents what you've just drawn from me.'

His mouth curved into an ironic little smile. 'You knew I'd understand, Kathryn. Not only do I share the background with Ric, but you were also privy to my own experience of something similar with Harriet Lowell.'

'Yes.' She forced her stiff mouth to return his smile. 'I guess that's it.'

There was an awkward silence—bad times swirling

between them, memories neither of them could easily dismiss. Kathryn was torn between wanting him to go and wanting him to make some approach to her on a personal level.

His hand lifted in a kind of apologetic appeal as his straight black brows lowered in a frown. 'I'm sorry this business with Ric resulted in...'

'Lateral damage?' she quickly supplied, hating his harking back to Jeremy. 'We've already established it would have been a bad mistake for me to marry Jeremy Haynes, so there's no point in referring back to it.' A rush of hot pride made her add, 'And I'd prefer you not to mention what I've just told you to Ric. It's over. Behind me.'

He nodded. 'No need for him to know. You can trust me to stay silent on that score, Kathryn.'

She did. 'Thank you.'

'Doesn't eliminate the hurt, though,' he said softly, sympathetically.

The heat in her cheeks grew more intense. Impossible to tell him he was far more attractive to her than Jeremy. In every sense. The hurt she was feeling now came from the futile yearning for Mitch Tyler to see *her* as a woman he could get attached to.

'I'm over it,' she stated insistently, fiercely rejecting his sympathy.

'Ready to move on,' he interpreted, his eyes challenging hers with an odd trace of whimsy that had the weird effect of curling her stomach.

'Yes,' she snapped, wishing *he'd* let the whole thing with Jeremy go.

'Want to test that?'

The question confused her. 'I beg your pardon?'

'Well, I really enjoyed your company on the one evening we spent together, Kathryn. I'm thinking…why not have that pleasure again? Providing you're up for it…with Jeremy planted firmly behind you.'

She stared at him in chaotic disbelief. Was he asking her out with him? Challenging her to prove she was moving on?

He smiled. It was a slow warm smile, his eyes teasing her out of any resistance. 'Now that we've got Ric sorted out, why don't we stroll around the quay, drop into one of the bars near the opera house, have a drink together, choose a restaurant for dinner— plenty of them along the concourse—and generally relax.'

He *was* asking her out with him!

It might only be a sympathy/empathy thing.

Maybe a reward for keeping faith with his friend.

A celebration that Ric's problems were now over.

A bit of mutual relaxation because the danger they'd both known and faced was gone.

She didn't care. Her heart was tap-dancing, shooting excitement through her whole body. Happy tingles banished all sense of caution. It might only be one night out with him but no way was she going to refuse it.

'I'd like that,' she said.

'Good!' He positively grinned, pleasure sparkling in his eyes. 'So grab your bag. Let's go and enjoy the evening.'

Enjoy…yes, she would. Just forget everything else

and enjoy being with him. There was no ring on her finger. She was free to follow her instincts and it was utterly impossible to repress the hope that they'd lead her somewhere good.

CHAPTER EIGHT

FOR Kathryn, it was a magical evening. Although there was the nip of approaching winter in the air, she was warmed by Mitch's company as they strolled along the concourse toward the opera house. A host of ferries were coming in and out of the quay to transport commuters home to their north shore destinations. The great Sydney Harbour Bridge that towered above the scene was buzzing with traffic. People were rushing all around them, but not she and Mitch. He was giving her his time and attention and Kathryn revelled in it.

It was easy to make conversation with him. She enjoyed listening to details of his life as a barrister, his description of various colourful personalities he'd met. He asked her about Ric's business, how she was dealing with her end of it in the absence of her boss.

He also made it easy to relax with him when they stopped at a bar and he insisted she have a fancy cocktail for fun. The talk gradually moved on to current affairs, personal likes and dislikes. There were no awkward moments. Everything felt like a natural progression.

They dined at a harbourside restaurant, both of them ordering oysters and the fish of the day, sharing a preference for seafood. She had no hesitation in drinking the fine chardonnay Mitch ordered with it.

It added to the happy intoxication of being with him and she didn't have to drive home.

Ever since moving to Bondi Junction she'd been catching the train to and from work—easier and faster than being trapped in peak hour road traffic. However, Mitch wouldn't allow her to catch a train home when their dinner was over, insisting on taking her in a taxi and seeing her safely to her door.

It was the act of a gentleman, she told herself, wary of reading too much into it, though he had shown every sign of taking pleasure in her company. She was even beginning to believe he *was* attracted to her. Would he have been so charming otherwise?

Quite a few times her heart had caught when his eyes had seemed to be simmering with more than casual warmth. But he'd made no move on her. No attempt to even hold her hand. And certainly no open suggestion of sexual interest. Yet, as he climbed into the taxi beside her, Kathryn was acutely aware of her own physical—sexual—response to him.

In fact, she was so conscious of it she concentrated very hard on getting the seat belt fastened properly so he wouldn't have to help her this time. Pride insisted that he not sense her vulnerability. So far he had given no indication that he actually wanted to pursue a relationship with her. This might only be a one-off night…an act of kindness, making her feel better about herself.

It was ending fairly early. Though it had started early, too. Five o'clock until ten o'clock was a considerable amount of time together. And he had to be on the ball in the courtroom tomorrow. A late night

Get FREE BOOKS and a FREE GIFT when you play the...

LAS VEGAS GAME

7

Just scratch off the gold box with a coin. Then check below to see the gifts you get!

YES! I have scratched off the gold box. Please send me my **2 FREE BOOKS** and **gift for which I qualify.** I understand that I am under no obligation to purchase any books as explained on the back of this card.

306 HDL DZ9V   106 HDL D2AC

FIRST NAME	LAST NAME

ADDRESS

APT.#	CITY

STATE/PROV.   ZIP/POSTAL CODE   (H-P-07/04)

7	7	7
🍒	🍒	🍒
🔔	🔔	☘

Worth TWO FREE BOOKS plus a BONUS Mystery Gift!

Worth TWO FREE BOOKS!

TRY AGAIN!

www.eHarlequin.com

Offer limited to one per household and not valid to current Harlequin Presents® subscribers. All orders subject to approval.

wouldn't be reasonable. Or was she making excuses because she hoped for so much more with this man?

Her nerves were wound up so tight she couldn't think of a thing to say. It was impossible to sound casually relaxed when she wasn't, anyway. The taxi left Circular Quay, heading up Macquarie Street. It would be fifteen minutes at most to Bondi Junction at this hour. Could she ask Mitch in for coffee? Would that be too forward, too suggestive, too *needy?*

They'd already had coffee.

She'd been out of the dating game so long, having been in an exclusive relationship for almost two years, she didn't know how it was played now. And Mitch Tyler was older, more mature than the men she had mixed with before Jeremy. Surely it was up to him to make a move…if he wanted to. Or was he waiting for some sign from her that she wanted continuance? If he thought she was still hurting over having to break her engagement…

Her fingers were fretting at her skirt. Realising they were betraying her nervousness, she consciously slackened the agitated movement just as Mitch reached across and took one of her hands in his, enveloping it in warmth and causing her heart to slam against the constriction of her tight chest.

'Thank you for what has been a very pleasurable evening, Kathryn,' he said with what sounded like deep sincerity.

Was it an exit line or…?

She had to chance a look at him.

He was smiling.

'I've enjoyed it too, Mitch,' she rushed out, her own mouth breaking into a hopeful smile.

'I was wondering…'

'Yes?' Did that sound too eager?

'You did say you liked classical music,' he went on smoothly. 'I have season tickets for the opera and an empty seat beside mine for the performance of La Bohème this coming Saturday night.'

An empty seat…that Harriet would have filled if they'd still been together?

But Harriet was out of his personal life, just as Jeremy was out of hers.

His eyes appealed for her acceptance as he added, 'We could take in a dinner first…or supper afterwards…'

Relief whooshed through her at what was definitely an invitation. 'I'd like that very much.' Was that too emphatic? She felt so giddy, controlling her response to him was beyond her.

'Good!' He grinned. 'Let's do the lot then. I'll pick you up at six, if that suits.'

'Six is fine. I'll be ready.'

She'd never been to an opera, didn't know if she'd like it or not, but she was ready to embrace any experience with Mitch Tyler. All her instincts said he was special. Very special.

During the rest of the taxi ride he told her that the La Bohème they were going to see was the new Baz Luhrmann production which updated the story to the 1950s—very revolutionary, and causing a sensation, making opera far more accessible to the general public—an experience not to be missed, he assured her.

Kathryn happily agreed, though she was far more aware of him holding onto her hand than what he was telling her.

He asked the driver to wait for him when the taxi pulled up outside the block of apartments where she lived. Which meant he was not going to linger over seeing her to her door. She didn't know if she was disappointed or relieved that he didn't expect to be invited into her home tonight.

Did he only want companionship from her?

He caught her hand again as he escorted her inside, causing her pulse-rate to zoom and her throat to tighten up, especially since he fell silent and she didn't know what he was thinking.

It was an old block of apartments, only three storeys high and no elevator. Kathryn couldn't afford anything fancy by herself. The rentals in Sydney were sky-high. The foyer was rather shabby and there was certainly no class about the concrete staircase that led up to her first floor apartment.

Was Mitch noting the obvious status comedown from her living with Jeremy? Or was he as preoccupied as she was with what could come next?

When she stopped at her door he released her hand so she could get her key out of her bag. 'Six o'clock Saturday,' he said as a reminder once the door was unlocked and opened.

'Yes.' She quickly smiled her pleasure in the arrangement.

'Good night, Kathryn.' He leaned down and planted a friendly kiss on her cheek.

The warm, tingly contact brought a tide of heat up

her throat. 'Good night, Mitch,' she replied somewhat breathlessly before he could see her becoming flushed. 'Thanks again.'

He nodded and she bolted into her apartment, closing the door and leaning back against it until her heart stopped pounding from the mad rush of excitement. Just a kiss on the cheek! How would she feel if he kissed her with passion?

Mitch returned to the taxi, elated that all his initiatives had paid off and relieved that he'd managed to maintain control over urges that might have screwed up the chance to start building a relationship with Kathryn. He was sure that patience would serve him better in the long run, given that she was still very sensitive about the break-up with Haynes.

Besides, he liked the idea of courting Kathryn in an old-fashioned manner. It had been all sex with Harriet, right from the beginning. Red-hot desire could blind a man to what he should be looking at. He wasn't going to make that mistake this time around, though how he was going to keep holding temptation at bay, he didn't know.

He got back in the taxi, gave his address to the driver and settled back for the ride. As the car pulled out from the kerb, Mitch's gaze was drawn to a man who was getting out of a BMW Roadster directly across the road, a streetlight shining down on his face.

Recognition hit him like a blow.

Jeremy Haynes!

He'd only seen him once before but he hadn't forgotten anything about the man—Kathryn rushing into his embrace, being swung around. Mitch had hated every second of it while the saner section of his mind had acknowledged the physical and material assets that had drawn Kathryn to the guy she'd been intent on marrying.

Past tense!

So what was Haynes doing here?

As the taxi accelerated, Mitch turned to watch Kathryn's ex-fiancé, tension ripping through him as Haynes headed straight for the block of apartments where she lived. Had he been sitting in his car, waiting, watching for her to come home? For what purpose?

It spelled trouble to Mitch.

It might be over for Kathryn but clearly it wasn't over for the guy she'd rejected. And Mitch didn't want what he'd established with Kathryn being messed around.

'Stop!' he hurled at the driver, aggression pumping through him at the thought of Kathryn being stalked. Of course Haynes wouldn't want to let her go. What man would?

'Forgotten something?' the driver quizzed, bringing the taxi to a halt.

Haynes was entering the building, moving fast. 'I've got to go back,' Mitch muttered, his sense of urgency screaming for action. He whipped out his wallet. 'What's the fare?'

'Want me to wait?'

'No.'

'Fare's just on fifteen dollars.'

Mitch handed him a twenty and bolted out of the

cab, racing back down the street, determined on running whatever interference was necessary to keep Kathryn on track with him and out of Haynes's clutches.

All his senses were on red alert as he strode into the foyer of the apartment block. He heard nothing coming from the first floor. No altercation. Nothing. The silence alarmed him even further. He raced up the stairs. Jeremy Haynes was not outside Kathryn's door.

Mitch paused at the top of the staircase, churning over what this had to mean.

She had let him into her apartment.

But why would she if she no longer wanted him in her life?

Harriet wouldn't have got past his door if she hadn't kept his key, letting herself in. There'd be no reason for Kathryn to give Haynes a key. She had to have let him in.

He forced his mind to sift through this highly disturbing situation. Haynes couldn't have been bothering Kathryn on any consistent basis. She had too much sense to invite trouble with him. This had to be a surprise visit, taking her off guard.

So why had he come now...after three months?

Time to let her stew over regrets, change her mind about sharing a future with him? Life in a penthouse apartment might be more attractive now that she'd had a lengthy taste of a less wealthy lifestyle.

Mitch dismissed that argument. Money wouldn't sway her.

So what argument could Haynes use to win her consideration?

And why choose tonight of all nights to try for a reconciliation?

Sheer coincidence?

No!

The realisation burst upon Mitch that the same news he had used to get to Kathryn could also be used by Haynes. Gary Chappel's death. Which had undoubtedly been reported on both radio and television by now.

Lara Chappel's safety was no longer an issue.

Haynes could argue there was no conflict of interests any more. He could apologise, say he'd been wrong, express intense regret at having sided with Chappel's pursuit of his wife, explain he'd been anxious about his career, wanting the best possible future for both of them.

Could he sell that argument to Kathryn?

Would she accept it?

Would she *want* to accept it?

Mitch wanted to believe she'd reject it, yet the long investment of emotional involvement with Haynes, to the point of a commitment to marry…impossible to be certain which way she'd jump.

It sickened him to think she was listening to the self-serving bastard, letting herself be persuaded, maybe even rushing back into his embrace as she had the last time Mitch had seen them together.

His hands clenched. He had to fight this. He couldn't bear to lose his chance with Kathryn now.

She'd given him positive encouragement. He was not about to give Jeremy Haynes any free ground with her.

He moved determinedly to her door and pressed the buzzer button beside it.

No response.

He jammed the button in with his thumb, frustration mounting, anger stirring. He knew she hadn't gone out again. What excuse could she have not to answer?

Again there was no response.

But he could hear movement inside the apartment. A thump. Then Kathryn's voice raised in panic. 'Stop! I don't want this. Let me up. Let me up.'

A muffled curse from Haynes.

Kathryn shrieking, 'No…! No!'

Mitch beat on the door with his fist, yelling, 'Open up! Open up or I'll call the police!'

More cursing. The door was wrenched open, Haynes glaring at Mitch, breathing whisky fumes as he jeered, 'It's just a domestic, for God's sake! Butt out!'

'No…it's not!' Kathryn cried from somewhere out of sight. She was gasping for breath, frightened, desperate.

Mitch put his shoulder to the closing door and barged in.

Knocked aside, Haynes grabbed at him in belligerent defence. 'Who the hell do you think you are!'

The words floated past the drumming in Mitch's ears. Kathryn was struggling to raise herself from the floor between a sofa and a coffee table that had been knocked over on its side. Her skirt was hitched up, her blouse askew, buttons ripped open.

'Mitch…' She lifted a pleading hand to him, her eyes huge with shock and fear.

'Get out!' Haynes shouted, trying to shove him.

The memory of Jenny's rape seized Mitch's mind. His sister…now another woman he cared deeply about being assaulted. Fury boiled up in him. Reaction came so fast he was barely conscious of violence erupting, his hand pushing Haynes to arm's length, his fist slamming into the lying face of the man who'd abused Kathryn's trust, Kathryn's body.

He felt the crunch of his knuckles hitting bone and it felt good. It felt right. Blood spurted from the slime's nose as he went down. Mitch grabbed him up by the collar and dragged him out of the apartment, down the stairs.

'Stop! Help! For God's sake!' the guy was whimpering.

'Shut up and thank your lucky stars I don't beat you to a pulp,' Mitch growled, barely repressing the urge to hurl him down the stairs, throw him into the street, rub his bloodied nose into the gutter so he'd remember the smell of filth, which was what he was.

Only the memory of months with Patrick Maguire stopped him. The old man's advice rolled through the red haze in his mind…control…discipline…put your energy into making the justice system work. All Mitch had achieved since he'd left Gundamurra would be wiped out if he was charged with another assault and convicted.

Yet the law wouldn't have saved Kathryn tonight.

The law wouldn't have got the chance because Haynes was stronger than she was. The law didn't rescue. It worked backwards, after a crime was committed. And then there were victims like Jenny, always carrying the memory.

Mitch grimly set Haynes on his feet in the foyer, then forcibly marched him out across the street to his big money car—the kind of big money that made some men think they could get away with anything. The guy was stumbling, moaning. Mitch didn't give a damn about his pain. The physical pain of a broken nose didn't last as long as emotional trauma, and God only knew what Kathryn was feeling.

They reached the driver's door of the BMW Roadster. 'Get out your keys and go,' Mitch commanded. 'If you ever think of bothering Kathryn again, remember me, and don't doubt for one second that I'll come after you and exact retribution. Understand?'

'Yes…yes…' Haynes sobbed, frantic to get away, the stuffing completely knocked out of him.

Mitch waited until he'd taken off, watching the car move out of sight as he headed back across the street. His body was a mass of jumping nerve-ends, his mind powering in all directions. He tried to calm himself down as he re-entered the building. He had to focus on Kathryn now, move carefully with her.

She hadn't even closed the door to her apartment. A bad sign. He walked in and found her huddled in a corner of the sofa, hugging her arms, looking shell-shocked. Her lovely green eyes were huge. No doubt his violence had added to her distress, but she *had* pleaded for his help, though not anticipating the form it had taken. He hadn't anticipated it, either. That punch had exploded from him.

'I packed him into his car and saw him off,' he stated, letting her know that any further threat from her ex-fiancé had been removed.

She shuddered.

Mitch spotted her suit-jacket and handbag lying on the armchair closest to the kitchenette, obviously dropped there before Haynes had arrived. *Why had she let him in?* Not the time for questions now.

He set the coffee table back on its legs, picked up the jacket and laid it on the table within easy reach if she wanted it for warmth. In her current fragile state, she might shrink from any physical contact from him, especially after seeing what *he* was capable of when stirred into action.

She didn't move.

'I…I thought it was you…at the door. That you'd forgotten…to tell me something,' she said shakily. 'He was in…before I could say no. Then…then…'

'It's all right, Kathryn,' he softly assured her. 'I'm here now. You're safe.'

She shuddered again. The chill of shock. Or fear. Maybe fear of him, too? But he couldn't just walk out and leave her like this. Yet how was he to give comfort without touching?

The jacket was probably inadequate for making her feel secure, protected. A blanket would be better.

It was a small, very basic apartment, the layout quickly scouted—one bedroom, bathroom, living room, kitchenette. He bundled a quilt off her bed and carried it out to the living room. Not daring to risk tucking it around her, he laid it across her lap so she could pick it up and snuggle under it.

'How…how did you know, Mitch?' Even her voice was trembling.

'I was leaving in the taxi when I saw him in the street, heading this way,' he answered matter-of-factly, exerting every bit of control he could muster to resist the rampant urge to grab her up and wrap her in his arms.

'And you…came back?' She finally lifted her gaze to his, her eyes still huge, intensely vulnerable, needing to understand, struggling to find her way out of the wilderness of what had happened.

Before he was aware of it, his hand was out, tenderly stroking her cheek, wanting to impart comfort and reassurance. 'You said it was over, Kathryn. I was worried Haynes might make a nuisance of himself.'

She dragged in a deep breath. 'Thank you. Thank you for coming back, Mitch.'

Relief…gratitude…nothing too negative there.

'I'll get you a hot drink,' he said, forcing himself away from her before he did something stupid.

He wanted her so badly—wanted to crush her to him, warm her body with his, kiss any memory of Haynes right out of her mind—but now was certainly not the time to make his desire for her known. Trust was the big issue here and now, and fraying any measure of trust would be a terribly wrong move. What he wanted might be very unwelcome.

It had to wait.

CHAPTER NINE

KATHRYN couldn't control the convulsive shivers that kept running through her. Her mind was still trying to grapple with the shock of Jeremy's virulence when she'd denied him any chance of a reconciliation.

Why he'd thought Gary Chappel's death would make any difference…it was all so unbelievable! No appreciation—no understanding—of what he'd revealed about himself or how she felt about it. His ego blinded him to any fault in his own attitude.

She was the unreasonable one.

Then his linking of her rejection of him to seeing her come home with another man, and the monstrous possessiveness that had ignored her right to say no…

If Mitch hadn't come back…

Thank God he had! Thank God!

All those assertions that she could take care of herself…impossible against a man intent on having his own way, taking it against all reason, forcing it. And the shock of it happening—the sheer disbelief—so paralysing.

Mitch had rescued her from…her mind shied away from the memory of Jeremy's forcing hands, his horribly marauding mouth.

She almost gagged.

It's over, over, over, she fiercely recited to herself. And Mitch was in her kitchenette, filling the electric kettle with water, preparing to make her a hot drink, looking after her. He'd been so gentle with her, bringing her the quilt from her bed, caring...yet he was so immensely strong...strong enough to knock Jeremy right off his feet, drag him out of the apartment, force him into his car and make him drive away.

Which definitely meant it was over. Jeremy wouldn't return to this apartment. He'd been beaten here, hauled away legless. He would hate any reminder of that humiliation. She was safe. Mitch had made her safe.

Strange that she didn't feel revolted by *his* act of violence...blood spurting from Jeremy's nose. Normally she would hate witnessing such a thing. It had shocked her, yet it had also been an enormous relief to have the whole ghastly situation ended in virtually a moment. Maybe there was a time and place for such primitive action. A slap to stop hysteria. A punch to stop aggression. Especially when the aggressor was taking rights that weren't his to take.

Anyway, she certainly didn't think any less of Mitch Tyler for doing it. In fact, she was intensely grateful to him for stepping in and taking Jeremy out. As for the rough handling of her ex-fiancé...good that Jeremy had a taste of that himself, having dealt it out to her.

Justice...

Though it was bitter.

How could she have been so blind about Jeremy? To even *believe* she loved a man who had no respect for the person she was! What did it say about her to

Mitch Tyler? He must think her a fool, completely lacking in any judgement of character.

She was consumed with shame, unable to look him in the eye when he brought her a cup of tea, setting it on the coffee table along with milk and sugar. It was an effort to even utter the words, 'Thank you.' She stayed huddled under the quilt, feeling too raw and exposed to move.

He settled on the armchair adjacent to the sofa. She felt his gaze on her, yet couldn't bring herself to look at his face, the expression in his eyes. The silence tore at her nerves. She was with a man whose good opinion she desperately wanted and her mind was a total mess, unable to function in any kind of positive frame. At least the warmth of the quilt had stopped the shivers but there was a cold empty place in her heart that yearned to be warmed by other means.

'Have I frightened you, Kathryn?'

The quiet question startled her into answering, 'No!'

A quick glance at him picked up his tension, the worried look that stabbed concern at her. It stirred confusion. Why would he think she was frightened of him?

'I'm not normally a violent man,' he explained, one of his hands lifting, opening in a gesture of appeal.

The hand that had punched Jeremy.

Of course.

What had gone down here tonight had to worry him.

He was a barrister, sworn to uphold the law, and hitting Jeremy could possibly get him disbarred. He'd put his professional career at risk for her sake, and here she was, totally focused on herself and how he must view her. At least she could help him on that point.

'I'll swear Jeremy was assaulting me if he goes to the police, Mitch,' she said with determined vigour, pushing her own misery aside. 'But I don't think he will. It would show him up as a loser and obviously—' she grimaced '—he'd do anything not to lose.'

'I wasn't thinking of him. Though I appreciate your offer to stand by my action. I meant...' He paused, his eyes searching hers with riveting intensity. 'My sister was raped a long time ago: It affected her...very deeply.'

'It didn't get that far,' Kathryn quickly assured him.

He nodded. 'Seeing you on the floor... I was remembering Jenny when I hit him. I know I lost control. It must have looked...savage to you. I felt... savage. But I want you to know...I don't go around bashing people on the spur of the moment.'

'I didn't imagine you did.'

'Violence is usually anathema to me,' he pressed on, clearly anxious to emphasise that point. 'I hate it in other people. I fight against it in court. Any form of abuse...'

'I'm sure you do.'

His eyes locked onto hers, driving home his point. 'I don't want you to be frightened of me.'

'I'm not,' she insisted. It was the absolute truth.

His relief was patent. 'I sensed you were withdraw-ing from me. I thought…'

'Not from fear.' She took a deep breath and un-loaded the burden on her heart. 'I'm just so ashamed…'

'There's no reason for you to be,' he shot back at her. 'It wasn't your fault.'

'But I chose him. I was going to marry him,' she burst out, shaking her head in anguish at the terrible mistake she'd made.

'Most of the time, people only let you see what they want you to see,' he argued. 'You were taken in by him, Kathryn, just as I was taken in by Harriet. Both of them very clever people.' His mouth relaxed, tilting into a wry smile. 'And both of them very at-tractive on the surface. A lot going for them.'

He was excusing her error, trying to lighten her sense of guilt, being kind. Her mind writhed over his kindness, knowing she should appreciate it but hating it. Hating it because brutal honesty would have been infinitely preferable. It would have told her he was feeling more for her than *kindness*.

'I glossed over things,' she muttered. It was what Mitch was doing now. For her sake. Wanting her to feel better.

'Don't we all gloss over things to keep relation-ships going?' He shook his head. 'Don't be so hard on yourself. Be glad that you're out of it. I think you're well rid of him.'

'No doubt about that,' she said with a mountain of feeling.

'Good! Then don't give him any more space in your thoughts.'

A derisive little laugh gurgled from her throat. 'That's not so easy.'

He hitched himself forward on the armchair, a pained look on his face, his eyes blazing with some strong emotion—anger, annoyance, frustration?

'Kathryn...don't fret over this. He's not *worth* any more of your time.' His voice was forceful, vibrant with the power of all the dynamic energy that emanated from him. 'And *your* value is not diminished because his golden image is in tatters,' he went on. 'You're a very desirable woman.'

'Am I?' Her own frustration welled up. She hurled the quilt aside, not wanting to feel she was Jeremy's *victim*. Not wanting to be treated like it, either, her hurt soothed by the one man she did want. Her feet swung to the floor and she stood up, bristling with the need to sweep aside all this *soothing* and face up to the real truth. She flung out her hands in sheer exasperation, appealing for straight honesty. 'Am I desirable to you?'

The words spilled from her agonised uncertainty. They weren't meant to be a challenge. But they put him so blatantly on the spot, acute embarrassment flooded through her with painful heat. She saw the shock on his face. Then he surged off the armchair so fast her vision blurred, and the next thing she knew, his arms were around her, drawing her hard against him—a distance-shattering impact that left her no room to back-pedal.

'You want to know how *intensely* desirable I find

you?' he challenged, his chest heaving against her breasts, his eyes searing hers with a desire so raw it took her breath away. 'I'm barely holding onto restraint, Kathryn. Barely holding on. I realise you're not ready for...'

'Not...ready?' she repeated incredulously. Everything within her was responding chaotically to this physical contact with him. It felt as though she'd been waiting her whole life to be held by Mitch Tyler, and to suddenly learn he'd been wanting her all along completely blew Kathryn's mind. Her inner angst tumbled out. 'I thought because of your connection to Ric and the business with Lara...both of us being at a loose end... I thought you were being kind to me.'

'*Kind?*' The word exploded from him as though he violently hated it. He sucked in a quick breath. His black brows beetled down. 'Is that what you want from me? No more than kindness? A friend in need?'

'No...no...' A wild recklessness whirled through the dizzy realisation that there was far more than friendly caring coming from him. Her hands moved from his broad shoulders, linking behind his neck. 'I want to experience all of you, Mitch Tyler.'

There! It was said.

And she didn't care that it had been said.

It was true.

Mitch's heart was pounding in his ears. Had he imagined what he needed to hear? Her mouth was still slightly parted, tempting him, inviting him. She'd put

her arms around his neck. She had to be willing...
ready...wanting...

He couldn't hold back. Couldn't. Desire was roaring through him. His mouth crashed down on hers and any seductive persuasion was completely beyond him. He kissed her with all the pent-up passion she'd stirred from the first moment they'd met, and amazingly, she gave it back, as though she, too, was consumed with an urgent, overwhelming need for him.

Her body was soft, pliant under his touch and his hands could not resist finding and learning every lovely curve of it, moving her closer, wanting the warm imprint of her stamped on him...*his woman*. Arousal came fast and hard but there was no withdrawal from her, no attempt to pull away. She was actually pressing herself against him, exciting him further, *wanting* him excited. Whether consciously or instinctively he didn't know.

Didn't want to know.

Didn't want to think.

Just wanted to absorb the feeling of her giving herself to him.

Kathryn could scarcely believe the tumult of feeling that was powering through her. Her mouth was tingling with excitement, revelling in the intense passion of his kisses, craving every erotic sensation he stirred. It was wild, wild and incredibly wonderful, intoxicatingly addictive.

And she loved the tensile strength of his body, the hard muscularity of his broad shoulders, his chest, his thighs, all of them encasing a dynamic energy that

seemed to be pouring into her, electrifying her own
vitality, pumping her heart faster, making it gallop
with sheer elation. No doubting his desire for her any
more. She felt his erection pressing against her stomach and exulted in the undeniable evidence of what
he was feeling.

Wanting her.

Needing her.

Drawing on her desire for him with dizzying intensity.

She'd never felt anything like this in her life.

His mouth moved from hers, his lips trailing across
her cheek. Panic clutched her mind as she thought he
was going to speak, to stop. But he didn't. He blew
into her ear, sending exquisite tingles right down to
the apex of her thighs. His tongue tantalised the sensitive whirls and he blew again, exciting a rush of
melting that made her body clench.

He felt the urgent tightening, drew back. 'Have I
gone too far?' His voice was furred, more self-
questioning than asking her but she answered him
with a fierce rejection of any withdrawal. 'No!' But
if they were going to make love, and that was what
she desperately wanted... 'Let's move to the bedroom, Mitch. Please?'

He sucked in a quick breath, tilted his head back,
eyes blazing into hers, a turmoil of questions. Her
stomach churned. It would be unbearable if he pulled
away now. Had she reminded him of Jeremy mauling
her in this room? She wanted to scream that it didn't
count. Only what he made her feel mattered and any-

thing less than the full experience of it would leave her in a dreadful limbo, wretchedly empty, deprived.

Driven to stop him from questioning further, she lifted herself on tiptoe, moved her hands to press his head down to hers and kissed him with all the fervour of her desire to hold him with her. His response was instant and gloriously satisfying, swamping her with the heat needed to expel the cold fear of being rejected. Her mind danced with feverish joy.

It was going to happen.

He wanted her every bit as much as she wanted him.

'Come with me, Mitch. Come with me,' she murmured against his lips, her heart beating like a drum roll of wild anticipation.

She grabbed his hand.

He came with her.

Into the bedroom.

She tore off the blouse Jeremy had ripped open, tossing it onto the floor with a shudder of distaste. She reached around to unclip her bra but other hands closed around her arms and drew them down, preventing her intention from being carried through. Her heart kicked in chaotic alarm. Had Mitch changed his mind?

Then he was kissing her shoulder, the warmth of his mouth chasing away the rash of goose bumps. 'This isn't a race, Kathryn,' he murmured. 'I won't just tumble you onto that bed and get it over with.'

She tensed. Was he having second thoughts?

Yet he was trailing kisses up the curve of her neck, mesmerising her into stillness with that same gentle blow of breath into her ear. 'I want you to know what you're doing.' Even the soft expulsion of his words was thrilling. 'Know it very consciously,' he went on. 'Not an impulse of the moment. And no regrets in the morning.'

'I won't regret it,' she promised huskily, barely able to catch her breath.

'Then you won't mind if I put the light on.'

The light!

Kathryn was instantly attacked by nerve-wracking doubts. What if Mitch didn't find her so *desirable* when he saw her undressed? In the naked light! She wasn't strikingly beautiful like Harriet. Her figure was more petite, her skin paler, freckled where she'd caught the sun. In the dark there'd just be feeling, everything centred on physical contact...man and woman wanting each other.

But if she protested, he'd think...he'd think she wasn't truly ready for him and she was. Her entire being was yearning for him. There was no choice...no choice at all as he lifted his mouth away from her ear, slid his hands caressingly from their hold on her arms, stepped back...

...and switched on the bedroom light!

CHAPTER TEN

KATHRYN felt like a rabbit, caught in the middle of a road, spotlighted by the bright beams of an oncoming car. She couldn't move. Her legs had turned to water, the muscles in them quivering like melting jelly. Only her spine stiffened, an instinctive reaction to feeling under threat. And her senses sharpened.

The room smelled stuffy from having the windows shut. At least it was tidy, the bed neatly made, though the quilt was gone and the pillows were slightly awry from its removal. Heat was rushing through her, scorching her cheeks, making her squirm inside. She heard the soft swish of clothes being removed. It jerked her head around.

Mitch was standing by the doorway, only a metre from where she remained rooted to the spot. His suit coat was gone. He was sliding his tie out from under his collar. But his eyes were on her, watching, burning with a sizzling challenge as he tossed the tie onto the coat which had already been dropped on the floor. His hands started flicking open the buttons on his shirt.

'Tell me to stop if you want me to, Kathryn.'

Stop? The word echoed around her mind, losing any meaning it might have had as her fascinated gaze clung to what was being revealed of his body. There *was* hair on his chest but not a lot—shaped like a T, running down to the waistband of his trousers, dipping below it to…she wanted to know, wanted to see, her own poignant sense of vulnerability overridden by a compulsion to have this intimate view of him.

He was so very powerfully built, the strongly muscular shoulders and arms emanating a *manliness* that grabbed at her heart—a man who could and would fight for her safety, the ultimate protector. Who was even now intent on protecting her from making an impulsive decision which might feel wrong in the morning.

Kathryn knew it wouldn't.

A man like Mitch Tyler was rare in this world. Not to experience all of him was unthinkable.

Shoes and socks gone.

She turned to face him, deliberately removing her bra to show him she had no intention of stopping anything. Her nipples instantly tightened into jutting hardness. He stood still, staring at her bared breasts. They were reasonably well shaped, if a little on the small side, Kathryn fiercely told herself, refusing to be daunted now, fighting the panicky feeling that she might not measure up to other women he'd had.

His broad chest expanded with a sharply indrawn breath. His gaze lifted to hers, glittering with determined purpose. 'Do I need to use a condom, Kathryn?'

Relief rushed through her. He still found her desirable. He wasn't going to stop. And she trusted him to be safe. He was a protector.

'No. I'm on the pill,' she answered quickly, recoiling from the idea of having any barrier between his flesh and hers. The contraceptive pills she'd been taking had kept her safe from pregnancy this past year. No need for anything else.

She kicked off her shoes, recklessly eager now for what was coming with Mitch Tyler.

He started unfastening his trousers.

Her hands whipped to the zipper at the back of her skirt, determined on matching his undressing, not letting any inhibitions telegraph uncertainty to him. *Intensely desirable,* he'd said. And *he* wasn't hesitating in stripping himself completely free of clothes. As long as she kept watching him, not thinking of herself, she'd be fine.

It was good that the light was on. Without it she wouldn't have been able to see the full length of him…magnificently naked. He was so beautifully male, his strong physique perfectly proportioned, every millimetre of him exuding dynamic virility.

And suddenly it was totally and gloriously irrelevant if her own body lacked some wonderfully stunning feminine allure. The sight of her—or the thought of her—had certainly triggered full sexual arousal in Mitch Tyler, his erection unashamedly blatant, wildly increasing her own excitement.

Yet still there were a few nerve-twanging moments as he simply looked at her, his gaze roving down over her tautly peaked breasts to the small triangle of auburn hair that hid her sex, lingering there, causing her inner muscles to contract at an uncontrollable rush of moist heat.

'You *are* magic,' he murmured, and moved slowly

toward her, shaking his head as though trying to free his mind from some spellbound state.

Kathryn shook her head, too, more in incredulous confusion. How could he associate magic with her? What did he mean by it? But there was no time to think. His arms were sliding around her waist and his body was closing in on hers—bare flesh contact—an explosion of sensation bursting through her. He held her tightly to him. She felt enveloped by his strength. Yet he was tender, too, rubbing his cheek gently over her hair.

'I want you to feel good about this, Kathryn.'

His caring for her, over and above his own physical urgency, reinforced all she knew of him, adding a special glow to what she was feeling. It wasn't just sexual attraction, not on her part, not on his, either. The connection went deeper, touching, filling the lonely emptiness in her heart.

'Let me make love to you,' he softly urged. 'Let me experience all that you are.'

The repetition of her own words swept away any sense of inhibition. There could be no holding back if they were ever to reach that mutual satisfaction. This was a time for giving whatever was asked. She tilted her head back to look into his eyes—eyes that bored straight through to her soul with their burning need—and instantly gave him her trust.

'Yes,' she whispered. Such a little word, yet it carried a mountain of consent, a mountain to be scaled however he chose, taking her with him.

His face broke into a smile, pleasure bursting from him, pleasure he transmitted to her mouth in a kiss that was more intent on tasting and exploring an escalating sense of intimacy than stirring an immediate and overwhelming passion. His restraint—control—was both tantalising and incredibly seductive.

He scooped her off her feet and carried her to the bed, his eyes gleaming wickedly as he said, 'You bring out the caveman in me, Kathryn Ledger.'

She laughed, bubbles of wild happiness dancing in her brain. If they were living in primitive times, she thought, sharing Mitch Tyler's cave would definitely be the best place to be in every sense…especially having him come home to her, sweeping her up in his arms, laying her down as he was doing now, hovering over her in all his magnificent maleness, poised to take possession, her own body brilliantly alive with anticipation, humming with joy because *she* was his pleasure.

If he'd taken her right there and then, she would have welcomed him with intense satisfaction, but she quickly realised he meant to keep her waiting, though not because he didn't want her. Desire poured through his fingertips as he caressed her arms, her legs, even her feet, touching with such exquisite sensitivity, following the touch with kisses, making love with a slow, gradual intensity that blew away all her previous experience.

Impossible to even feel shy about what he was doing, not when he looked so entranced with how she felt to him, so completely absorbed in every womanly aspect of her. It gave her the glorious sense of being incredibly special, precious, faultless, even beautiful. The way he kissed her breasts—drawing them into his mouth, tasting, licking, the slow rhythmic suction building an almost feverish pitch of excitement—completely erased any thought of them being anything but loved by him. Adored by him.

And when he moved down to do the same to her clitoris, Kathryn was totally swamped with waves of ecstatic pleasure, driven to fantastic peaks of excitement with the accompanying caress of fingers that knew exactly where to touch and when and how. She had never been made love to like this, not with such awesome, *knowing* sensuality. And she couldn't wait any longer to feel him inside her…this amazing, wonderful man who could stir her entire being into craving him so intensely.

'Please… I need you now,' she cried, grabbing at his arms, frantically urging him to fulfil this last ultimate need.

He responded instantly, and her own body arched in sheer euphoria as the surging power of his own desire—held back for so long—met hers and plunged forward, filling the aching void, reaching her innermost self, fusing with it. And having achieved that marvellous union, he paused there, letting her savour the bliss of it as he bent down and kissed her, taking her mouth on the same sensational journey of merging with him, increasing the sense of deep intimacy, stirring a passionate yearning for it to go on and on.

She wanted to make love to him, to let him know how she felt about him. She glided her hands up and down his back, over his buttocks, her fingers tracing the tense muscles, finding the erotic zones below his hips. It propelled him into moving, his body rocking over hers as he drove each rhythmic thrust to a thrilling depth, and she wound her legs around his thighs and swung her own body to meet his, squeezing her muscles around him, heightening the delicious friction, and her fingers raked through the hair on his chest, up and down, up and down, inciting the fast action that would bring him to climax.

She could feel his heart pounding, matching the wild beat of her own, and inside her the ripples of pleasure growing more and more intense, white-hot excitement melting around him as he took them both to the pinnacle of absolute bliss—the sweet surrender of all control to a fulfilment that was uniquely theirs, the two of them one in brilliant harmony.

Then just holding each other, savouring the contentment of being so close, intertwined, sharing themselves in a warm silence that needed no other communication, the sense of completion leaving no space for wondering about anything. She lay with her head resting just under his chin. His hand idly stroked her hair.

Eventually her mind admitted the odd train of thought and she smiled over one of them. 'You won't ever have to club me over the head, Mitch.'

'Why would I want to club you over the head?' he asked, sounding helplessly bemused.

'Caveman…taking his woman.'

He laughed and rolled her onto her back, propping himself up one elbow to smile down at her. 'Are you telling me you'd always be willing?'

'Hmm…*always* is a big word,' she teased, although her mind was singing *yes*. She reached out and stroked his cheek, feeling the slight bristle that shadowed his jawline, finding it very masculine and sexy. 'I would expect you to listen to me.'

'I have very good hearing,' he assured her.

'Very good everything.'

'Is that so?'

'I feel extremely fortunate to be with you.'

'Indeed.' He grinned. 'I'm feeling rather lucky myself at the moment. Kind of like Peter Pan. Completely rejuvenated. Must be all your fairy sparkles still swirling around me.'

'Fairy sparkles?'

'I look at you and think…Tinkerbell.'

'You don't!' She laughed at the fanciful thought.

'I do.' He silenced her laughter by grazing his fingers lightly over her lips. His eyes simmered with teasing pleasure as he added, 'A very alluring Tinkerbell. It's the red hair and green eyes, this beguiling mouth that promises a whole world of secret treasure, and the petite perfection of your femininity, right down to your dainty feet. Plus the most provocatively sexy ears I've ever seen.'

He bent down and blew his sexy magic into the ear closest to him, and Kathryn held her breath as the incredibly erotic sensation stirred all her nerve-ends into skittish excitement. It whizzed through her mind that she'd never curse her pixie ears again. If they turned Mitch Tyler on, she was positively blessed with them, especially when what he was moved to do was a madly electric turn-on for her.

It was on the tip of her tongue to say Harriet Lowell

had to be brain-dead to allow any other man to supplant him in her bed.

A swift instinctive caution zapped the dangerous comment. Reminding him of his ex-lover would be just as horribly intrusive as reminding him of her ex-fiancé.

This was between them.

Which made it different.

And to her, it was a million times better than anything she'd had with Jeremy. She hoped Mitch felt the same way. *If* he was comparing it to what he'd had with Harriet. A jealous sense of possessiveness drove her onto her side, pressing closer to him as she slid her arm around his back and played her fingers over the tautly delineated muscles that were so much a part of his intrinsic masculinity.

This man was hers tonight, she thought.

How they would fare together in the future she had no idea, aware there was still a lot to learn about each other, but she would never ever regret the experience of this night with him. He had made her feel good about herself. More than good. And she didn't believe it was just *kindness,* though it had followed fast on the heels of Jeremy's gross behaviour with her.

She lifted her face to his and he kissed her.

The quick rise of passion was promise enough that this was no one-night stand.

Not for him.

And certainly not for her.

CHAPTER ELEVEN

A month later...

AS USUAL, his clerk handed Mitch a sheaf of messages once court had been adjourned for the day. The top one simply read 'Call Johnny' and gave the telephone number—a *local* number. The afternoon's legal arguments were instantly banished from Mitch's mind. Johnny Ellis was back in town.

He started smiling and the smile grew into a happy grin by the time he was out of the courthouse and calling the number on his mobile telephone. Johnny had been in the U.S. for the past five months, recording an album and doing a tour, and no doubt he was on his way home to Gundamurra, just stopping off to catch up with Mitch and Ric as he always did when he could.

Johnny...the entertainer. And no doubt his nickname in the music industry—Johnny Charm—was well earned. Back when they were boys at Gundamurra, it was he who had invariably lightened any dark moments with his unquenchable good humour. Not to mention the songs he could make up about anything. Even then he'd been brilliant on the guitar Patrick had given him.

A hotel receptionist answered his call and connected him to the man himself. 'Hey, Mitch!' The big voice boomed over the line. 'Do you happen to be free tonight?'

'Where and when?'

'Thought we'd join up at the Italian restaurant under Ric's apartment at Woolloomooloo. *Otto's*. Seven o'clock suit you?'

'Fine! Have you been in touch with Ric yet?'

'Tried at his company office. His chief assistant told me he'd gone out to a lunch appointment and hadn't come back. I'll give his home number a buzz at five o'clock, see if he's there.'

'Do that. See you soon, Johnny.'

Mitch's pleasurable anticipation in the get-together dimmed somewhat as Ric's current situation played through his mind. Gary Chappel was dead, Lara and Ric were both back in Sydney, but she was shying clear of him, using the excuse of the funeral and the publicity around her husband's death in her request for him to stay away from her—a request that had been delivered through Mitch.

And Ric was hurting from it. Badly. He was desperate for face-to-face contact with her. No doubt his heart was still very much engaged there. Almost obsessively so. Kathryn had commented that he wasn't on top of his work at all, his mind very much elsewhere. A whole month had gone by and still no direct word from Lara.

Mitch wondered if he should word Johnny up so he didn't touch on painful areas tonight. Ric had borrowed his plane for the getaway. But if that was brought up it could be quickly skated over and Ric wouldn't like it if Johnny treated him with any special sensitivity. He still had that chip on his shoulder from the old days—a dark wounded pride that drove him beyond where most men would go.

And Mitch was certain now that Lara was at the core of it.

Beautiful, damaged Lara, who was currently taking the steps to put the past behind her, and the hell of it was, Ric had probably become too much a part of that past.

Deep emotional baggage.

Mitch shook his head over it as his clerk waved him to the taxi waiting at the kerb, ready to take them both back to his chambers. As he settled into the car for the short trip, he was wondering how much emotional baggage Kathryn was still carrying from her relationship with Haynes.

Since that first night together, she hadn't once referred back to it, not in all the time they'd spent in each other's company. And he certainly hadn't wanted to remind her. The revelation that Haynes's ambition had no moral boundaries had clearly been a big shock, undermining her confidence in her ability to judge people. His subsequent bullish attempt to claim her back had rattled it even further, causing a complete loss of faith in herself.

At least Mitch had managed to restore a good chunk of that.

And won her trust.

But shame was an insidious thing.

Had she managed to bury it or did it still haunt her?

Was she throwing herself into this affair with him

because she wanted him…or because she *needed* him to exorcise the ghosts Haynes had left her with?

Mitch grimaced over his abandoned plan for an old-fashioned courtship. A slow build-up to intimacy would have assured him that what they shared had nothing to do with a rebound effect. As it was…well, it had been totally impossible to reject Kathryn's need that night, especially when he'd been so pumped up from getting rid of Haynes and wanting her himself.

Having taken that step, it was equally impossible to retreat from it. Every time he was with her, whatever they'd decide to do—the opera, a concert, a film, lunch, dinner—it was only a preliminary to satisfying the desire that leapt between them the moment they met and kept simmering to the moment they ended up in bed. Not even making it to a bed sometimes.

Sex was insidious, too. It was such a dominant force—the constant seduction of intense pleasure. Did Kathryn look beyond it when she was with him? How much did she care for the person he was—apart from being the lover who made her feel good?

Time, he assured himself, would eventually answer that question.

It had only been a month.

A month of hell for Rie, which was patently obvious when he joined Mitch and Johnny at *Otto's* for their night out together. He wore the grim look of a man who'd been taken to the brink of total devastation and he was only just hanging onto his determination to survive. Dead man walking, Mitch thought.

Though he did warm up as the evening progressed. Johnny exuded a bonhomie that was irresistible, regaling them with tales from his country and western music world, and Mitch kept the wine flowing. There was a lull in the conversation when Johnny took off to the men's room and Ric's whole demeanour drooped, making it very clear that the effort to maintain a cheerful countenance was draining him.

'Still nothing from Lara?' Mitch asked sympathetically.

A derisive flash from bleak dark eyes. 'As a matter of fact, I met her for lunch today.'

'Not good news?'

His mouth twisted. 'Thank you and goodbye. And nothing I said made a jot of difference.'

'Maybe more time…'

He shook his head. 'Got to put it behind me, Mitch. I'll be off to New York at the end of the week.'

'She did have a hell of a life with Chappel. I can't go into detail…'

'No. It's finished. Let it go.'

The terse finality left Mitch with nothing to say. He knew Ric would hate sympathy yet he keenly felt the death of his friend's eighteen-year dream. He well remembered the nights at Gundamurra when Ric had talked of his Lara, like she was the embodiment of all a guy could ever want in a girl.

It was a sobering reminder to Mitch that a deeply felt attachment did not guarantee a life of togetherness. Timing and circumstances could be big factors in whether or not a happy outcome was reached.

'I hear you've linked up with Kathryn.'

The comment jerked Mitch out of his old memories. 'Yes,' he answered briefly, not wanting to explain how, when and why.

'She's a good person.'

'Yes, she is.'

Curiosity flickered through the dull flatness of Ric's eyes. 'Did she break her engagement because of meeting you, Mitch?'

'No.' He wished it had been so. 'It was a personal issue between her and her fiancé,' he added, not wanting Ric to think it was some fallout from his business with Lara. His friend already had enough grief to deal with. 'I didn't know she'd broken up with him until the day of Chappel's death.'

'Well, at least that's a clean start for you,' Ric muttered.

Mitch didn't disillusion him.

It wouldn't help Ric and it wouldn't help the situation he had with Kathryn.

Johnny returned to the table and the talk moved on to Gundamurra. 'Haven't been home since last Christmas. What about you guys?' Johnny asked.

'I made a flying visit, end of February,' Ric answered casually, no hint that it had been on an extraordinary mission. 'Borrowed your plane, Johnny.'

Johnny grinned. 'Bet you enjoyed flying it, Ric.'

He nodded. 'A real pleasure.'

'And you, Mitch?'

'Haven't had the time.'

Johnny wagged a finger at him. 'You make time this coming Christmas, hear? All three of us together. I know your sister had a new baby last year—fair enough—but this year…no excuses! I'm laying down the law.'

'Getting too big for his boots, isn't he, Ric?' Mitch teased, passing off the pressure of decision, not knowing where he'd be with Kathryn and suspecting it would be a long time before Ric would want to return to Gundamurra and memories of Lara.

'It's all his country and western music and being in the U.S. too long,' Ric quickly chimed in. 'Thinks he's a cowboy now, able to ride roughshod over both of us.'

'Watch it, brothers,' Johnny mock-threatened. 'I'm bigger than both of you.'

The old camaraderie carried them through the rest of the evening. Ric caught the elevator up to his apartment, leaving Johnny and Mitch to catch taxis to their separate destinations. Though they ended up walking to Johnny's hotel, while Mitch explained why, as Johnny put it, 'Ric looks like he's been through a wringer and hung out to dry.'

Best that he knew before arriving at Gundamurra tomorrow, Mitch thought. Patrick would want to know how the situation had panned out, too, given his close involvement with it.

'So he took her home and it didn't work,' Johnny commented sadly.

Home…it was how Johnny always referred to Gundamurra. To him, Patrick was the father he'd never had before, caring about him enough to listen to his dreams and help them come true, telling him he was always welcome at the outback sheep station where their future lives had been shaped. Mitch still had family, but Johnny and Ric had no-one. It meant a lot to them that Patrick had offered his home as their home…their safe place in an ever-changing world. They counted on him being there for them, knowing who they were, liking and respecting the men they had become.

Mitch left Johnny at his hotel, wishing him a safe flight to Gundamurra tomorrow, and took a taxi to Woollahra. As he walked into the home he had made for himself, he was thinking he was different to Ric and Johnny. He'd had a mother who'd loved him, a sister who remained very much a good part of his life. Yet Patrick had still been important to him, too— Patrick and what he'd taught them and brought out in them at Gundamurra.

Mitch knew those six months when he was sixteen were an integral part of who he was now. And Kathryn didn't know that part of him—didn't know what he'd shared with Ric and Johnny, didn't know he had, in fact, been convicted of assault. She only knew what he'd chosen to reveal to her, and even if that did win her heart, he knew that in the long run, everything would need to be told, for his own satisfaction that what she felt for him was real…and solid.

Johnny's comment kept running through his mind. *So he took her home and it didn't work.*

When Christmas came this year, would Kathryn accompany him to Gundamurra?

And if she did…learning the darker part of his life…would their relationship still work?

CHAPTER TWELVE

Two months later…

'I NOW pronounce you husband and wife.' The marriage celebrant paused to smile before adding, 'You may now kiss the bride.'

Ric swept Lara into his embrace and the love beaming from their faces brought tears to Kathryn's eyes. Somehow, it was all the more moving because she and Mitch were the only witnesses to this very private wedding.

Lara was over six months pregnant, with Ric's child, not Gary Chappel's as she had feared. The DNA test had relieved her of any further concern on that score. Thank God! Kathryn thought, having seen Ric's torment over Lara's initial rejection of any further involvement with him. If Johnny Ellis hadn't gone to Gundamurra and found out about Lara's pregnancy before Ric had taken off to New York…

'It did work,' Mitch murmured.

'What?' Kathryn whispered, still watching the passionate clinch of the newly married couple and envying the absolute certainty of their love for each other.

'He took her home. And it worked for them,' Mitch answered, nodding at some private satisfaction in his mind.

It touched a highly nervous chord in Kathryn. Once they saw Ric and Lara off on their honeymoon, *she* was taking Mitch home to Gosford with her—his first meeting with her parents—and she couldn't help feeling apprehensive about it.

There had been no real decision made about this step. She'd mentioned it was her mother's birthday this weekend and she was expected home for it. Mitch had said he might as well use the time to visit his sister at Green Point, and since that area was in the vicinity of Gosford, they could travel together in his car, with him dropping Kathryn off and picking her up on the way back.

Given the intimacy of their relationship, it would have sounded dreadfully rude to reject the offer—equally rude not to invite him into her parental home. Yet she felt horribly self-conscious about the visit, knowing how curious her parents would be to meet the man who had supplanted Jeremy in her life, probably wondering if she'd end up being hurt by him, too.

Mitch had accepted the invitation to dine with them tonight but he had stuck with his plan to stay with his sister, possibly sensing Kathryn's inhibitions about sharing a room with him under her parents' roof. Stupid really, given they could barely keep their hands off each other, but her parents didn't know that and she didn't want them to think she was plunging headlong into *another mistake*.

While it had been three very hot and heavy months with Mitch now, and there was no sign of his desire for her abating, Kathryn couldn't help thinking it was all too good—*magic,* as Mitch had called it—and the spell might break. Introducing him to her parents was a scary prospect, especially after getting to the point of planning a wedding with Jeremy.

Maybe Mitch didn't want the open commitment of sleeping in her parents' home, either, keeping his sister as an escape route to slide away when it suited him. Three months...it wasn't a long time, yet Kathryn couldn't imagine ever wanting to be with any other man. She hoped Mitch felt the same way about her. But he hadn't said he loved her, hadn't invited her to meet his sister, and here she was, taking him home with her.

Would it work for them?

He need not have come. He could easily have avoided it altogether instead of offering to drive her both ways. Maybe he was curious about her home life, wanting some more knowledge of her and her background. But what about him and his sister...who had been raped? They had never talked about that.

Because of Jeremy?

It dawned on Kathryn that she'd been floating along in a bubble of happiness where Mitch was concerned, but other things existed outside that bubble. There was nothing hidden between Ric and Lara any more and that was how it should be...everything known, accepted, understood. That was how it had to be for a marriage to work, with love underpinning it all.

She hadn't known enough about Jeremy, hadn't understood, and couldn't accept his attitudes when she had understood. Mitch Tyler was a very different person and she loved everything she knew about him, yet how much more was there she didn't know?

This was weighing heavily on her mind by the time they'd farewelled Ric and Lara. By then it was mid-afternoon, and since she and Mitch had decided to leave the city early to avoid peak hour traffic, their weekend bags were already in his car—nothing to delay their departure. They were very quickly on their way to Gosford, Mitch in the driver's seat in more ways than one, Kathryn thought.

Had he deliberately manoeuvred a meeting with her parents for some kind of check on her while still holding himself aloof where his own family was concerned? Her uncertainty about his intentions kept her tense and silent as the car headed north.

'I guess you're thinking of the wedding you didn't have.'

The comment startled her—the wedding forgotten, the focus of her thoughts entirely on the destination they were travelling toward. Even more startling—unnerving—was the mocking little smile Mitch flashed at her, especially when there wasn't even a hint of a smile in his eyes. The twin blue laser beams bit into her with hard, purposeful intent.

Kathryn's mind instantly clicked to red alert. This was Mitch's first reference to Jeremy since he'd forcefully taken him out of her life. It appalled her that he might think she regretted her ex-fiancé's departure...for any reason at all.

'I can't imagine anything worse than a wedding where there's no real love,' she said emphatically. 'I was actually envying Ric and Lara. They didn't need any flashy frills to make their wedding into *a big day*. Having each other was more than big enough for them.'

'Would you be content with a ceremony as simple as that?'

She hesitated, frowning. 'My family would be hurt if they were excluded.'

'So what they think is important to you.'

'Yes, it is.'

Another stabbing glance. 'What did they think of Haynes?'

Kathryn's breath caught at the directness of the question. Was Mitch worrying about how he would compare in her parents' eyes? 'They didn't really take to him,' she answered honestly. 'I thought it was…different lifestyles.'

'Are you worried about what they'll think of me?'

Her chest tightened up as her mind whirled through the concerns that had been nagging her. 'Why do you want to meet them, Mitch?' she burst out. 'What's this all about?'

His hands tightened on the steering wheel, knuckles gleaming white. His jaw looked clenched, too, his mouth thinning into a grim, determined line. Kathryn was acutely aware of strong emotion being barely contained. Yet when he spoke it was in a calm, measured tone.

'I'd like to know why you *don't* want me to meet them, Kathryn.'

She winced, hating the idea of explaining her reluctance to expose where she was now with him. Yet if she didn't…what was he thinking? That she was

ashamed of their relationship, not prepared to acknowledge it? Treating him like a gigolo who supplied her with sex—a person she didn't want to introduce to her parents because the relationship wasn't
serious to her? In actual fact, it was so serious, she
didn't want anything tainting it. But how to explain
that?

'It hasn't anything to do with you, Mitch,' she
plunged in, anxious to clear the air of anything offen-
sive or insulting. 'I foisted Jeremy on them and they
accepted him for my sake, while all the time they
worried that my marriage to him would turn out
badly. Though they didn't say that until after...after
I broke off the engagement.'

She took a deep breath as she struggled to clarify
the conflict in her mind. 'It made me feel worse that
they'd seen what I didn't. And here you are—' her
hands fluttered in helpless appeal '—driving a classy
Jaguar, exuding success, bristling with sex appeal,
and they'll think I've fallen for the same package
again—you taking over Jeremy's place.'

The ensuing silence felt as though it was loaded
with explosives. Kathryn closed her eyes, fiercely
hoping she hadn't just ruined everything with her own
squirmish guilt for being a blind fool.

'Am I the same package to you?'

Again his tone was calm, almost matter-of-fact, yet
the impact of his question sent shock waves through
her entire body.

'No!' Her heart sank at the train of thought she'd
planted in his mind. She shot him an agonised glance.
'You must know you're so much more, Mitch.'

He didn't answer immediately and his gaze remained fixed on the traffic, making it impossible for her to read his expression. She waited, literally on pins and needles, and when he did reply, it was indirect, putting her on the spot again.

'Then don't you think your parents are capable of sorting that out for themselves?'

His logic could not be refuted. Yet it didn't stop Kathryn from feeling intensely vulnerable about this meeting. 'You didn't answer my question,' she blurted out, needing more than ever to understand his intentions. 'Why do you want to meet my parents?'

He shrugged. 'Because you didn't ask me to. Just the flat announcement that you were off to be with them this weekend.'

A rejection by omission.

A little chill ran down her spine.

They'd been so close these past three months. Of course he'd wonder why she hadn't invited him to go with her. So he'd subtly forced a meeting. No waiting around on a back-step for Mitch Tyler. He went after what he wanted. Yet how *serious* was he about their relationship?

'You haven't asked me to meet your sister,' she pointed out. 'Why don't you do that, Mitch?'

'I was coming to it.' He sliced her a look that sizzled with challenge. 'Jenny would like you to join us for lunch on Sunday, if you can spare the time from your own family.'

He'd already planned it! It was sensing *her* reservations about being accompanied by him to her parents' home that had stopped him from delivering the invitation. She heaved a rueful sigh, realising she'd made a mess of what should have been simple.

'I have no problem with openly declaring an interest in you, Kathryn,' he went on. 'And I don't like being cast in the role of secret lover—kept hidden from your family. I'd much prefer you to feel happy about our relationship. Proud to have me with you.'

'I am!' she cried, horrified at how he had interpreted her nagging sense of failure over Jeremy. 'I'll be very happy to come to lunch with you and your sister's family on Sunday. Please thank her for the invitation.'

He nodded and said no more. But there was no smile from him, nothing to reassure her that he was satisfied with the situation.

Kathryn stewed over what he'd said all the way to Wahroonga where they turned onto the freeway and the travelling would be much faster. She had to get these issues settled before they reached Gosford. If this awful tension in the car was carried into the meeting with her parents, it would go dreadfully wrong. And it was her fault.

'Not inviting you to spend this weekend with me was not about hiding you from my parents, Mitch,' she stated emphatically.

'Good! Because I'm not about to let you, Kathryn,' he said with a hard, ruthless bite that alarmed her even further.

'What does that mean?' she snapped, instantly imagining him claiming intimacy with her in front of her parents…laying their affair out right on the mat, defying her to deny it in any shape or form.

'It means that I won't back off from meeting your parents and I don't give a damn if they spend the whole time comparing me to Haynes because I know I'm a better man than he is.' His eyes stabbed at her apparent lack of confidence in that point as he added, 'I thought you did, too, Kathryn.'

He returned his gaze to the road they were travelling, leaving her to sort out the confused mess in her mind. The really awful truth was she had been proud of Jeremy, happy to show him off as her partner. Which damned her as a superficial idiot. Mitch's sister didn't know that, which gave Kathryn a clean slate to work on, whereas in her parents' eyes…but she was thinking of herself, not Mitch. She wasn't being fair to the person he was—a far better man than Jeremy in every sense.

'I do know that, Mitch,' she said quietly, hoping he would forgive the offence she had clearly given.

He sighed, grimaced. 'I don't want to feel you've taken up with me on the rebound, Kathryn. That I'm fighting ghosts at every turn. You took off his ring but he's still there in your mind, influencing what you do—and don't do—with me.'

On the rebound…

That wasn't true. She'd been strongly drawn to the man he was before she'd broken up with Jeremy. But seeing Harriet Lowell in his home that first night had made her think the attraction couldn't be mutual. It was only when he'd openly said he found her very desirable—and proved it—that she could fully believe he actually *wanted* to pursue a relationship with her.

But that issue had all been triggered by the horrible

scene with Jeremy, so she could see how Mitch might think that making love with him—then and there—had been an impulsive rebound decision, driven by the need to wipe out the nastiness and supplant it with good feelings. And these past few months with him had been centred on the incredibly wonderful sex they had together. She'd wanted to wallow in it, not think ahead, just let it be.

It seemed...*dangerous*...to think ahead, to even consider a future together. She realised now that she felt *safe* within their relationship as long as it was kept to the two of them. In fact, she *had* subconsciously cast him as her secret lover, clinging to the intimacy of that privateness, not wanting any outside influence to threaten it.

She looked down at her bare left hand. The solitaire diamond ring was gone but what had happened with Jeremy *was* still in her mind. She had to get over it, let it go, or she might lose the man she most desperately didn't want to lose.

'Remember the day we met in your chambers?' she said, determined on changing his view of her feelings for him.

'Vividly,' he answered dryly.

'You affected me so deeply, it made me question whether it was right to go ahead and marry Jeremy. I was still questioning when you took me home the next night. Then Jeremy confirmed how wrong it was. So what I feel with you is not a rebound thing, Mitch. It started before there was anything to rebound from.'

Silence.

Did he believe her?

He was staring straight ahead as though focusing all his attention on the road but she could feel his inner tension as he weighed what she'd said against his own impressions of their first meeting. Kathryn worried over how many times he'd felt *rejected* by her, how much it was eating into him.

A sense of panic hit her as she realised they'd turned off the Sydney to Newcastle Freeway and were heading down the Kariong hill to Gosford. Another ten minutes and they'd be at her parents' home, where she hadn't made him feel welcome. Frantic for him to understand her motivation, she tried to explain further.

'I don't know if you've ever thought of marrying anyone, but it's not a commitment I walked into lightly and I couldn't walk out of it lightly. Having met you, I questioned my choice, but the questioning was painful and I wanted Jeremy to make the pain go away. But he didn't. He made it worse.'

'Fair enough,' came the relieving acceptance of her argument.

Kathryn was just beginning to breathe easier when he hit her with another question.

'You say meeting me caused you to question your choice. You knew I was unattached, so after you'd ended it with Haynes, why didn't you call me, Kathryn? You could have used any number of pretexts to contact me and let me know you were free. As it was, if I hadn't come to you...'

'Oh, right!' she exploded in frustration. 'Here's this powerful man who took care of me for a day because his old friend asked him to. And while I'm in his home, this beautiful tall blonde turns up—a barrister, as well, sharing his profession and clearly having shared his bed. Okay, so he says it's over. Do I look like Harriet Lowell? Do I share his legal world? All I am is an obligation he carried out with charming civility.'

He frowned. 'Did I make you feel like an obligation?'

She sighed at the hopeless error in her reasoning. 'No. You made me feel... I wished I wasn't engaged to Jeremy.'

'I was barely holding onto being *honourable,* Kathryn.'

The black irony of that statement squeezed her heart. He'd wanted her then. Wanted her all along. And she was not answering his need to feel wanted by her.

'I'm sorry, Mitch. Believe me, I thought of calling you many times. But having made such a huge mistake with Jeremy, I just couldn't...open myself to another hurtful mistake. I guess I'm a coward.'

'No. You helped Ric and stood up to Gary Chappel. You fought the big fight over Lara's right to safe refuge while your dreams were crumbling around you. And you walked away from all Haynes offered. Those are not the acts of a coward.'

A red traffic light forced a stop and Mitch reached out and enfolded one of her hands in his. Her gaze instantly sought his, begging forgiveness. 'I do want you with me, Mitch.'

And finally he smiled. It was slow and a touch wry,

but at least it was a smile that lifted some of the weight off her heart.

'You'll have to forgive me my black and white mentality, Kathryn. I'm not good at greys,' he said on a dry, whimsical note.

The traffic started moving forward again and Mitch released her hand, returning his to the driving wheel, leaving her with the tingling memory of its warmth and strength. The hand that had hit Jeremy, she thought, rescuing her, fighting for her.

It was now up to her to fight for him, to give him very positive signals because there was much on the line this weekend. No doubt about that. Her parents, his sister...there was no place for any negativity in either meeting. No place for muddly *greys,* either. Kathryn had the very strong sense that this was make or break time in her relationship with Mitch Tyler.

She wanted it to work.

The very thought of losing him...

No. She had to get her head straight once and for all. Mitch Tyler was *her man.* Somehow she had to make him believe she was *his woman.*

CHAPTER THIRTEEN

11.30 a.m. Sunday...

FOR Kathryn, the weekend had dragged almost un-
bearably since Mitch had left on Friday night. The
meeting with her parents had gone particularly well,
and when she'd accompanied him out to his car to
see him off, he'd kissed her with such passion, it had
hurt to let him go. She should have trusted what they
had together instead of worrying how her parents
might view it.

At least this lunch with his sister today gave her
the chance to show *his* trust wasn't misplaced.
Somehow she would show Jenny that Mitch was not
just an attractive package to her, but the man she
wanted at her side because he was incredibly special.

'Mitch is here!' her father called from the living
room. 'I'll carry your bag out to his car, Kathryn. Say
hello.'

She turned anxiously to her mother who was sitting
on her bed, watching her last-minute application of
fresh lipstick. 'Do I look all right, Mum?'

'Lovely, dear.' She smiled approvingly. 'That knit-
ted jacket looks brilliant on you. Very clever design
with all the different blocks of green.'

'Not too dressy on top of jeans? It's a barbecue
lunch. Mitch said casual.'

'It's classy casual. Not out of place,' came the decisive reassurance.

Kathryn took a deep breath to settle her madly accelerated pulse-rate and picked up her handbag, ready to go.

Her mother rose from the bed and linked arms with her, smiling indulgently and patting her hand. 'Stop worrying, Kathryn. It's perfectly obvious that Mitch Tyler cares about you. His sister will pick up on that and act accordingly.'

'But I want her to like me...for me.'

'Then just relax and be yourself. Come on. I'll walk you out to the car. Say hello to Mitch, too.'

'You do really like him. You're not just pretending for my sake.'

'Kathryn...' Her eyes were warm, glowing with pleasure. 'He's the best birthday present you could have brought me. I can now stop worrying about you. He's a good man.'

'Much better than Jeremy,' she pressed.

'Chalk and cheese,' her mother declared emphatically. 'Both your father and I feel...intensely relieved and happy for you.'

Mitch had been right. Her parents had had no problem perceiving the differences between the two men. It had been foolish of her to fret over their response to *this choice*. Black and white.

'Kathryn tells me you play chess,' her father was saying as she and her mother emerged from the house. 'We'll have to have a game next time you come.'

'A pleasure I'll look forward to,' Mitch answered, smiling, looking totally relaxed with the situation.

Next time.

Kathryn's heart skittered with the happy hope that everything was all right. Mitch had forgiven her for casting him in the role of secret lover. Their relationship was out in the open now—doubly open with its being acknowledged in front of her parents and his sister.

He looked spectacularly handsome, his magnificent physique clothed in blue jeans and a royal-blue skivvy, their colour reflected vividly in his eyes, his strong face as beautifully masculine as the rest of him. Her whole body yearned for contact with him, but he was holding the passenger door open for her, and conscious of her parents watching, she simply smiled her pleasure in his company as she got in the car.

Once they were on their way, Mitch reached across and took her hand, instantly imparting a warm reassurance in their togetherness. 'Just to clear up any doubts that are festering in your mind,' he drawled, casting her a purposeful glance that raised flutters in her stomach. 'I have not taken Harriet Lowell nor any other woman to meet my sister, so you're not about to be subjected to any comparisons, Kathryn.'

'Oh!' Relief surged through her, followed by the stunning realisation that he was letting her further into his life than he had ever allowed anyone else. Which made her squirm even more over her own reservations about introducing him to her parents.

'Mitch, I am sorry about my…my misgivings. Mum and Dad think you're great,' she declared, hoping that resolved the problem she'd raised.

He smiled with a touch of irony. 'So I passed muster.'

'With flying colours,' she assured him.

'They're good people, your parents,' he said seriously. 'They care about you, Kathryn. As they should.'

It reminded her that Mitch's own father had not cared, walking out on him and Jenny, leaving a disabled wife behind, too. A really terrible desertion. Then Jenny getting raped...some horrible man not caring about what he was doing to her, taking what he wanted. Like Jeremy. Only much, much worse.

'Is your sister okay, Mitch?' she asked impulsively.

He sliced her a querying look. 'Why do you ask?'

'You told me...the night you rescued me from Jeremy...you said Jenny had once been raped,' she recalled hesitantly, wondering if she was treading on highly sensitive ground.

'That was when she was eighteen, Kathryn. She's thirty-six now, very happily married, and we don't talk about that time,' he stated firmly, flashing her a look of warning. 'It's long in the past,' he went on. 'She loves her husband, adores her two children and she's looking forward to meeting you.'

Which all proved true over the next couple of hours. Kathryn instantly warmed to Jenny and her husband, Hal, both of them very welcoming and easy to chat with. Their three-year-old daughter was a very cute charmer, all over her 'Uncle Mish' who indulgently gave the attention she demanded of him. He'd be a good father, Kathryn thought, watching him cradle his nine-month-old nephew in the crook of his arm, and talking to him as though the baby understood everything he said.

Hal and Mitch cooked prawns and swordfish steaks on the barbecue, sharing the children between them while Jenny invited Kathryn to help her with salads in the kitchen, having already prepared a big potato bake with cheese and bacon. It was a friendly open plan house with lots of sunlight coming in. A happy house, Kathryn thought, taking Mitch's point that his sister had long moved on from old traumas.

They ate lunch out on a large covered deck overlooking a sparkling inground swimming pool, and the atmosphere was so relaxed, Kathryn thoroughly enjoyed herself. She had no premonition of what was to come after the children were put to bed for an afternoon nap.

The men did the clearing up from the barbecue and Jenny led her down to a lounge setting near the pool, saying they might as well soak up the sunshine while they could. It was a glorious spring day, perfect for being outdoors. They settled down with mugs of coffee, and Kathryn wasn't surprised when Jenny used the opportunity to learn more about her.

'Mitch tells me you're Ric Donato's executive assistant in his Sydney office,' came the casual opening.

'Yes. I guess you must know Ric since he and Mitch are old friends.'

'I know of him. I've never met him.'

That did surprise her. 'You've never met?'

Jenny shook her head and grimaced. 'It goes back to Gundamurra, you see. Mitch was sent there because of me. And that's where he met Ric and Johnny Ellis.'

'Sent there…because of you?' Kathryn was intrigued. It was certainly a piece of background information Mitch had never offered. She swung her feet off the lounge, sitting on the side of it to face his sister who suddenly looked very uncomfortable about having imparted it.

'I thought you knew.' Her eyes searched Kathryn's anxiously. 'Working so closely with Ric…being with Mitch…'

Sensing retreat and eager to persuade Jenny to reveal more, she quickly offered, 'All I know is that Ric took Lara—the woman he's just married—to Gundamurra to keep her safe from her husband. It's an outback sheep station and I gathered that Mitch has been there himself. Johnny Ellis, too.'

Jenny bit her lips and stared into space for several minutes. 'He keeps protecting me, but he can't protect me from my guilt,' she finally muttered.

Definitely a reference to her brother, Kathryn thought, knowing how strong Mitch was on protection. But what was he protecting his sister from now?

'What guilt do you have, Jenny?' she asked softly, wondering if it was related back to the rape that Mitch said they never talked about.

She shook her head but was also frowning as though struggling with a decision, possibly torn between personal need and loyalty to her brother. Kathryn didn't press, sensitive to the fact she had no right to dig into what was none of her business. Curiosity could be taken only so far, especially on such short acquaintance. Better that Jenny didn't tell her anything she might regret letting out. Kathryn wanted her friendship more than she wanted information.

She sipped from her mug of coffee, trying to think of something to say that would ease the tension emanating from Mitch's sister. Jenny was a much softer person than her brother, not the female equivalent at all. She was very feminine, very pretty, with warm brown eyes and curly brown hair and a naturally giving nature. It was easy to see that she would have been a generous carer to her mother, a wonderful nurse, and now a very understanding wife to a busy doctor. Easy to also see she was the kind of person who would stir a powerful protective instinct in her brother.

'I want to know. I *have* to know.'

It sounded like a desperate decision, jolting Kathryn out of her own train of thought and focusing her very acute attention on Jenny as she turned to her, the lovely brown eyes dark and pained.

'How can I help?' The words spilled from Kathryn, her sympathy instantly aroused.

It triggered an outburst of angst. 'When I heard the news reports of Gary Chappel's death…in a plane crash at Gundamurra…and one newspaper said Mitch was acting for Lara Chappel… I knew it had to be all connected. I just knew. But Mitch will fob me off if I ask him. So will you tell me, Kathryn? You must know what went on.'

She had no idea what the connection was in Jenny's mind but clearly Mitch's sister was deeply disturbed by it. There seemed no reason not to tell her the whole story, beginning with the photograph that suggested Lara Chappel was the victim of physical abuse from her husband, what Ric had done about it, how Mitch had handled the legal end, then after Gary Chappel's death, Lara's withdrawal from Ric until Johnny Ellis had gone to Gundamurra and found out about her pregnancy, the DNA test which had proved Ric was the father...

'...and they got married on Friday. Mitch and I were the witnesses,' she finished.

'Did Lara look happy?' Jenny questioned anxiously.

'Blissfully happy,' Kathryn assured her. 'It was abundantly clear that she and Ric love each other very deeply.'

Jenny sighed as though that knowledge gave her some relief. 'Ric's Lara,' she murmured. 'And all three of them contributing to that end after all these years.'

Her words instantly recalled other words Kathryn had heard spoken, Mitch talking on the telephone to Ric at Gundamurra, speaking in a very gentle, sympathetic tone—*Patrick said...this is your Lara...from the old days.*

'Would you mind explaining that to me, Jenny?' she pleaded, feeling left out of something she *should* know.

Jenny took a deep breath and spilled out, 'I'm a coward, Kathryn. That's why Mitch hasn't told you. Always protecting me. I never faced up to it, you see.'

'I'm sorry. I don't see.'

She grimaced. 'When I was eighteen I was brutally raped, and I couldn't bear to testify about it in court…couldn't bear to face the man again.'

'I can understand that. I'm sure Mitch did, too.'

'Yes, but…Mitch couldn't let it go. Couldn't bear that the man should get away with what he'd done. He went after him and delivered…rough justice. He was charged with assault and I didn't…couldn't bring myself to stand up in court and testify why he'd done it. Not then. And Mitch wouldn't say. Wouldn't bring my name into it. For my sake. So he was convicted and given the choice of spending a year in a detention centre or working six months on an outback sheep station.'

'Gundamurra.'

She nodded. 'The man who owns it, Patrick Maguire, had some special program going, wanting to help boys who'd run off the rails. Ric Donato and Johnny Ellis made the same choice at the same time. They were all sixteen. Ric had stolen a car, wanting to impress his girlfriend, Lara. Johnny had been caught dealing in marijuana.'

She paused, again anxiously searching Kathryn's eyes. 'You will keep this confidential, won't you? I don't think any of them would want this background to be public knowledge. Johnny's famous now. And Ric's very respectable. As for Mitch…'

'I promise you this information is safe with me, Jenny,' she returned earnestly.

'I made Mitch tell me everything about Gundamurra. I felt so guilty about him being sent there. He swore it was a good experience, that Patrick

Maguire had been like a father to them, and there'd been nothing bad about being with Ric and Johnny, either. Ric was a dyed-in-the-wool romantic who mooned a lot about some girl called Lara, and Johnny was fantastic at making up songs, playing guitar.'

'Well, that must have been true because they've been friends ever since,' Kathryn pointed out.

'Yes. And eventually, years later, when Mitch wanted to study law, I did go to a court hearing to testify on his behalf and his conviction was overturned. I could put it all behind me then. I felt it wouldn't come back to haunt me anymore.'

'Nor should it, Jenny. All these recent happenings have nothing to do with you.'

'But they do, Kathryn.' The haunted look in her eyes poignantly underlined her feelings, however misplaced they were. 'I might have saved Ric's Lara a lot of grief,' she added, clearly unloading the burden of guilt that weighed so heavily on her, yet it made no sense to Kathryn.

'I'm sorry. I don't understand how you could have done that. You didn't know…'

'It was Gary Chappel who raped me,' she cried.

Kathryn felt her heart recoil in shock.

This was the connection. The ramifications bounced around her mind as Jenny poured out her grief.

'He sucked me in with his good looks and charm. And he drove a Lamborghini. I was dazzled by him. But by the time he finished with me I knew what he was really like. The things he did to me…' She shook her head, distressed by the memories even now. 'I never told. And I should have done. A man like that…of course, he'd do it to others. He should have been charged. Put away. Mitch would have stood up and done it, but I…I let my brother be put away instead.' Tears welled and spilled down her cheeks. 'And Gary Chappel went on to hurt Ric's Lara.'

'Jenny—' Kathryn reached out and took her hand, squeezing it to impart some comfort '—it's not as black and white as that.'

Perhaps it was to Mitch—possibly why he and his sister never talked about this. But there *were* many greys in the way the world operated. Too many times there was one law for the rich who could buy the best defence, and one for the poor who had to trust they'd be believed.

'The Chappel family is mega-wealthy, Jenny. Victor Chappel would have done everything possible to get his son and heir off a rape charge, including tearing you to shreds on the witness stand. I'm sure Mitch is well aware of that. The way he handled Lara's situation…he knew what he was dealing with and how to bring pressure to bear on their response to it. But that's now. He couldn't have done that eighteen years ago. As you said, he was only sixteen, and I'm sure whatever justice he took into his own hands, he was willing to pay for. You know that, don't you? And Gundamurra wasn't bad for him. You know that, too. You shouldn't feel guilty about any of this.'

'But what about Lara? And there were probably other women…'

'I think for men like Gary Chappel, with great wealth behind them, only death is going to stop them from following their own bent. And he is dead, Jenny. It's over. Over for Lara, too. She's got Ric now and Ric is a really good person. Believe me, I know. I'm sure his love will make up for anything Lara suffered at her husband's hands. And maybe they would never have come together again if he hadn't seen that photograph. So it's really okay. You don't have to worry or feel guilty. Lara's fine.'

Jenny dragged in deep breaths and dashed the tears from her cheeks with her hand, blinked hard to clear her eyes. 'I've always felt wrong about it. Wrong about what I didn't do,' she choked out.

Kathryn knew only too well the shame she'd felt over her huge error of judgement in accepting Jeremy as the man she would marry. Jenny's shame was rooted in a much more dreadful trauma and stirred her deepest compassion.

'Don't feel wrong any more,' she urged. 'You were the victim of what was done to you, Jenny. It wasn't your fault. And it wasn't cowardly not to take on Gary Chappel yourself. I met him very briefly when he came to the office, chasing Ric and Lara. I would have been very frightened if I'd been his target.'

'He had no heart…no pity… I couldn't bear to be anywhere near him again.'

'Mitch wouldn't have wanted you to be. The moment I gave him Gary Chappel's name he had security guards sent to the office to protect me and accompany me to his chambers.'

The bleak memories in Jenny's eyes gave way to a spark of interest. 'You didn't tell me about that.'

'It's how we met.'

Kathryn ran on at considerable length, explaining how Mitch had taken her home with him that night to ensure her safety, adding that he considered Gary Chappel a dangerous psychopath with the resources to get his own way, whatever it took.

'So you see, Jenny, your brother doesn't blame you for anything because he knows the kind of man Gary Chappel was. And you shouldn't blame yourself, either,' she finished with conviction.

Jenny gave her a bemused look. 'So you two met because of him.'

And re-met because of his death, Kathryn thought, but she'd said enough to put the whole set of circumstances into reasonable perspective and Mitch's sister seemed to be considerably less stressed now. She smiled as she answered, 'Yes, we did. And I've got to say, Jenny, your brother is one hell of an impressive guy.'

It drew a smile from her. 'I think he's very impressed with you, Kathryn. In fact, you're the only woman he's ever brought to meet me. I thought it meant...' She gave an awkward shrug. 'I guess he's still protecting me...not telling you about Gary Chappel and Gundamurra. Thank you for...for setting my mind at rest.'

'Put it behind you now, Jenny,' she quickly advised. 'You have a great husband, two beautiful children, Lara is with Ric...'

'And Mitch is with you,' she cut in, sounding very satisfied with that outcome.

But he wouldn't have been with her this weekend if he hadn't pushed for it—all because *she* hadn't put

Jeremy behind her. Taking the diamond ring off wasn't enough. She'd made Mitch feel he was fighting ghosts at every turn and that wasn't right, wasn't fair.

Ghosts!

The realisation suddenly struck how very personal those ghosts were to Mitch. Hugely personal!

She'd told him Jeremy—the man she'd committed herself to marrying—had sided with Gary Chappel—the man who'd raped his sister, who'd subjected Ric's Lara to untold abuse...

Then on the night of the very same day she'd told him it was over, he'd seen Jeremy entering her apartment building. What must have been going through his mind when he followed...then found her ex-fiancé forcing himself on her...remembering Jenny's rape, hitting Jeremy as he had surely hit Gary Chappel, feeling intense violence toward both men?

Ghosts...and the long link to Gundamurra where Ric had taken Lara, bringing the past very much to the fore, memories he didn't talk about.

And *she* had thrown Jeremy in his face again because of feeling vulnerable about the meeting between Mitch and her parents. Jeremy, whom Mitch would judge to be in the same class as Gary Chappel! Black and white!

Am I the same package to you? he'd asked.

Dear God! The offence was horrific.

She remembered his tension in the car, the sense of violent emotion being barely contained, his white-knuckled grip on the steering wheel.

Yet despite all that, he'd asked her to forgive him

for *not being good at greys,* then followed up by completely charming her parents. And today...well, Jenny certainly believed Mitch thought she was special—the only woman he'd ever brought to meet her.

'I'm glad he met you, Kathryn.' Jenny was looking at her as though she answered more than she had already answered. 'Mitch has walked alone for too long. And he has such a big heart...so much love to give. You'll never find a more caring man.' She smiled her own love for her brother. 'Mitch cares with a passion.'

'I know,' Kathryn murmured.

And she did know.

It summed up all her experience of Mitch Tyler.

Yet she had to hear it from his sister to recognise its absolute truth.

It made her feel small, unworthy of him, but she silently vowed he wouldn't feel alone ever again.

He had rescued her from so much.

Tonight she would rescue him from all he'd kept to himself.

CHAPTER FOURTEEN

MITCH felt a happy sense of satisfaction as he drove away from his sister's home. Jenny's parting words, whispered as he kissed her goodbye—'She's lovely, Mitch. So right for you.'—and Kathryn sitting beside him now with an air of relaxed contentment…the uncertainties that had plagued him had been largely lifted.

Jenny had felt the magic.

Kathryn's parents had, too.

And the cloud Haynes had left on Kathryn's mind had been dispelled.

He felt far more confident now that he was winning the woman he wanted. Three more months to consolidate their relationship, then…he had to do it…had to take her to Gundamurra for Christmas. He hoped that being there would help her understand, meeting Patrick, feeling how that wise old man of the land and the immense space of the outback had taught him the futility of burning up with anger.

Far better for the explosive energy to be channelled into constructive purpose—achieving, not destroying, pursuing positive outcomes, not giving in to negativity. He'd done that, ever since he'd left Gundamurra. But he had snapped with Haynes, his fist flying out, connecting. Would Kathryn tie that to his earlier assault on Gary Chappel and worry about his capacity for violence? Would she be able to justify it in her mind, let it go, love him...without reservation?

'Thank you for taking me to meet Jenny and her family, Mitch.'

She was smiling at him, her beautiful green eyes lit with gold sparkles. His heart lifted, soaring with hope. 'Jenny thinks you're lovely,' he informed her, returning the smile.

'So is she. And Hal. And the children.'

'I'm glad you had a good time with them.'

'Very good. In lots of ways.'

He threw her a quizzical glance. 'Want to elaborate on that?'

She grimaced but her eyes held apologetic appeal. 'It hammered home what a fool I'd been to worry about this weekend.'

'New steps always carry uncertainties,' he said, knowing the feeling all too well.

'You know what the worst thing about it has been?'

'No. Tell me the worst.'

'Not having you with me all the time.'

It jolted his gaze from the road. Heat was flooding into her cheeks. There was a vulnerable look in her eyes, wanting him to agree, afraid he might not.

'I missed you, too, Kathryn,' he assured her. 'In fact, I was severely tempted to crash your mother's birthday party yesterday.'

'You would have been welcome, Mitch. I would have loved to have you there. We would all have welcomed you,' she said with a fervour that left no room for doubt.

'It's okay.' He reached over and took her hand in

his. 'We're together now.' Much more so than on the trip from Sydney, he thought, which was eloquent proof that controlling his anger over Haynes and arguing it through to a winning situation had earned him the result he'd aimed for.

Her other hand covered his, transmitting a desire for more contact with him, instantly arousing the strong sexual urge she'd always stirred in him.

'I want you to stay with me tonight, Mitch.'

His whole body clamoured for instant gratification. His mind dictated that waiting for the right time had to be enforced. Though it was impossible to keep the anticipation of it from simmering through his smile as he answered, 'I was hoping you'd want that, Kathryn.'

She laughed, a delightful gurgle of nervous pleasure.

Mitch wasn't sure how they made it back to Sydney. His driving had to have been on automatic pilot because he only became aware of the outside world when he brought the Jaguar to a halt in front of Kathryn's apartment building at Bondi Junction.

He managed to remember her bag…carried it for her.

She had the key to her apartment ready in her hand, unlocking the door with barely a pause.

They were inside.

He dropped the bag on the floor.

She flung her arms around his neck, her body rocketing against his, and the hunger for her he'd kept contained all weekend exploded through him. He kissed her, needing to draw her into him. His hands took their own urgent fill of her, roving greedily, possessively, over every delectable curve of her femininity, wanting the affirmation that she was his.

They tore off their clothes, her need as pressing as his, exciting him to a wild exhilaration. The caveman in him swung into action, scooping her off her feet, carrying her to the bedroom, and she was laughing with the mad rush of feeling, loving it, kissing him with joy, her hands running over him, inciting him to take her, intensely immediate.

He could not have waited anyway. She wound her legs around his hips, raising her body to meet the thrust of his, arching from the sheer ecstatic pleasure of instant satisfaction, the thrill of her response driving him hard and fast to the centre of her being. He wanted to feel her innermost self embracing him, engulfing, possessing, claiming her man.

It was awesome the feeling she gave him…the sense of utter euphoria. It ignited all the pent-up energy of the past few days and they rocked together in a wild, exultant rhythm, soaring to the crests of waves of excitement, wallowing in the shallows of voluptuous sensuality, revelling in every nuance of pleasure, loving each other.

It went beyond the physical. Mitch was sure of it. It wasn't just a sexual merging. He could see it in her eyes…the total giving of herself, becoming one with him, belonging together. And when he finally climaxed, a sigh of sweet fulfilment whispered from her lips, a sigh that rippled through her entire body, telling him she felt complete in every sense with him.

He hugged her close, savouring this new level of

intimacy, believing in it so strongly he wouldn't let himself think anything other than she felt it, too. It had to be. Right from the beginning he'd known instinctively she was the one. And she'd admitted being drawn to him, too, at their first meeting, drawn into wishing she wasn't wearing another man's ring.

He'd buy her a ring.

Not a diamond.

Something that would be special to her.

'Mitch…'

'Mmm…?' He smiled as her fingers played with the hair on his chest, twining it between them, surely another sign of her liking the sense of being joined with him.

'Jenny told me about Gary Chappel and Gundamurra.'

And his heart stopped.

Kathryn instantly felt the tight stillness of his chest. She was lying with her head resting on it, her ear close to the pleasant drumbeat of his heart—a heart fully relaxed from all tension. The beat was suddenly suspended. And the steady rhythm of his breathing came to a dead halt.

Shock, she thought, tingles of alarm racing through her brain. She hitched herself up to plead for his understanding, her eyes frantically trying to break through the glassy stare of his. 'I didn't bring up the rape, Mitch. I swear it. It was Jenny, wanting to know about Gary Chappel and Lara. And it just all came out because she needed to…to put everything together. I had to help her, Mitch. She was so deeply distressed…'

The shock in his eyes gave way to appalled disbelief. 'Jenny...' The name was expelled with the trapped breath released from his lungs. It carried the sound of some completely unanticipated betrayal.

Thinking he was hurt by his sister's choice to confide in her rather than the brother who cared so much, she quickly tried to explain Jenny's reasoning. 'It was the guilt thing, Mitch. She didn't want to lay it on you because she knows you don't want her to feel guilty. And neither she should. I think I convinced her of that in the end.'

'Guilt...' he repeated, seeming to struggle with taking that concept in.

'About not charging Gary Chappel with what he'd done to her, not testifying in court for you, letting you be sent to Gundamurra, then Ric's Lara being abused by the same man who should have been put away instead of going free to hurt other women.'

He stared at her with intense concentration, saying nothing. Kathryn thought he was waiting for more, perhaps still questioning why Jenny had unloaded all this on her instead of him. Deciding it was probably best to recount the whole conversation, how it had happened, she explained that Jenny had thought she knew everything because of her working with Ric and being with her brother.

'I understand what your sister then told me was private stuff, Mitch,' she went on anxiously, acutely aware of how tense he still was. 'But I thought it was more important to help than back off.'

*   *   *

Private stuff…

Mitch could barely get his mind around the shock of Jenny letting it all out to Kathryn, not just her life but his, too. *His,* too, before he was ready to deal with it. Without any thought of how it might impact on his relationship with Kathryn.

Yet as he listened to how the conversation had occurred, it sickened him that he hadn't realised… hadn't answered his sister's need. Chappel was dead. To his mind, that had ended it. Yet it was very clear now why Jenny had connected to Lara's situation. And Kathryn's arguments to assuage all the guilt were good arguments. Mitch doubted he could have done better himself, and possibly they were more cogent to Jenny, coming from an outsider looking at the situation objectively.

She's lovely.

An accolade well earned.

He knew he should feel relief that his sister's angst had been so comprehensively settled, should feel grateful to the woman who'd done it. But he felt raw—exposed—not knowing what Kathryn felt about his assault on Chappel, whether she'd linked it to how he'd dealt with Haynes.

Reason told him that she couldn't have made love with him if she had any negative feelings about what he'd done. Did this mean she had justified it all in her mind? Or was it all too fresh for her to assess properly, and the emotional time she'd spent with Jenny had spilled over into a desire to assuage his needs, too?

She was looking to him now for a response to all she'd told him, her lovely eyes troubled because of his silence. He was at a total loss for what to say, acutely conscious that she'd left out any comment on his actions and their outcome.

'I'm sorry if you feel I've intruded on what was none of my business, Mitch.'

'Jenny gave you no choice,' he acknowledged, hearing the terse note in his voice, unable to repress the tension coursing through him. All he could think of was he'd needed more time with Kathryn…more time…

'Does it matter…that I know?'

He forced himself to open up the big question in his mind. 'I guess that depends on whether it matters to you.'

'It gives me a better understanding of where you're coming from, Mitch.'

'What? A juvenile jailbird?' he mocked, wishing he could erase the memory of the violent rage that had once possessed him beyond all reason.

She now knew about Gundamurra, why he had been sent there. He'd disciplined the anger but it still grabbed him when injustices piled up, clawing at him. Even with Kathryn, giving more time to a man like Haynes when she was with him, putting her memories of that relationship ahead of what they had together.

'I don't think Gundamurra was a jail for you,' she said quietly. 'I think it gave you space…from where you were in your life.'

Space…yes. Space enough to make a big difference to where his life might have headed without Patrick Maguire's guidance.

'But I wasn't referring to your time at Gundamurra, Mitch,' she went on. 'I meant your…personal involvement with Gary Chappel.'

The assault.

He was not going to excuse it. Pain had been dealt out and pain had been dealt back. He did not regret that act. Never had. Though he didn't want to ever lose control of his own humanity again.

She dragged in a deep breath. Mitch found himself holding his, waiting for her judgement on him.

'I'm so sorry about letting Jeremy get in the way of your meeting my parents, Mitch. That was very wrong of me. Considering how he sided with the man who'd raped your sister, and tried to force me…it must have made you feel…'

Violent.

He'd wanted Kathryn to be his from the moment they'd met. And he'd forced himself to act honourably while she was hung up on a man who knew no honour. Where was the justice in that?

'Knowing what I do now,' she said ruefully, 'it must have been very difficult for you to be as you were…with me and my parents on Friday night.'

He'd been fighting for her. It seemed he'd been fighting for her all along. And right now he felt as though the mat had been swept out from under him, leaving him with no control over the outcome.

'I wish…with all my heart…I hadn't made it that way for you, Mitch. It wasn't fair.'

Nothing fair in love and war, he thought savagely. The old adages always held truth. Justice is blind…

'Please forgive me.'

He shook his head. 'There's nothing to forgive. You were being honest with me.'

'If I'd known the background…'

'It would have put a pressure on you I didn't want you to have. Nor do I want you to have it now,' he added fiercely. 'Trying to make up for something that had nothing to do with you.'

'Can't I care about what effect it's had on you, Mitch?'

His jaw clenched. What *effect* was she talking about? Did she think he needed the past raked over like Jenny? Guilt removed? He felt no guilt. 'Kathryn, I've been handling things since I was a boy. What makes you think I can't handle anything that's thrown at me?'

She heaved a long sigh. 'You can. And you do. You handle everything…brilliantly. Except…all this I've learnt today… I feel it goes right to the heart of the man you are…and you've shut me out of it…going it alone.'

Alone…

That one word hit so many chords, vibrating down the years to when he was a little boy starting school, trying to adjust to the fact that being too bright was unacceptable, that being able to read when others hadn't even begun to learn made him separate from them, a target to be beaten in other ways.

Alone and frightened when his mother was hospitalised for months and his father drank himself into a stupor every night, leaving him and Jenny to keep the household running for when their mother came home. Then when his father had deserted all three of them, the lonely responsibility of earning whatever he could so they could make ends meet, ensuring that bills were paid and whatever needed fixing was fixed.

No-one to lean on. No-one to *share* what he'd had to do. The closest he'd come to a sense of sharing was at Gundamurra, though he'd been different to Ric and Johnny, having a family who wanted him back, needed him back. But his mother was gone now. And Jenny... Jenny had turned to Kathryn, not him.

Kathryn...who was sliding down, resting her head on his chest, half-covering him, an arm around his waist, inserting a leg between his. 'You have such a big heart, Mitch,' she murmured, kissing him, trailing her mouth over where that very heart was beating with painful intensity. 'And I love you for it.'

She *loved* him?

'But I want you to let me into it. Not keep things from me any more. Give me the chance to handle them, too.'

She had handled them!

She wasn't worried about anything he'd done!

His hand lifted and stroked her hair, needing to reassure himself this wasn't a dream. It was real and he had to make a response that would satisfy her. His voice came out furred with a turbulent mix of emotion.

'I'm sorry...sorry I didn't tell you about Chappel from the start, but you were wearing another man's ring and I thought…' He could breathe easily again. He even laughed. 'It doesn't matter what I thought.'

In a surge of exhilarating energy, he rolled Kathryn onto her back and leaned over her, needing her to look into his eyes, know he was speaking with genuine sincerity. Deep sincerity.

'Thank you for what you did for Jenny. And you are very much in my heart, Kathryn. I just wasn't ready to open the doors you crashed through today, but I'm glad they're open now. Even more glad of the compassion and understanding you've shown over what has been revealed.'

Happy relief shone back at him. She stroked his cheek, touching, reaching into him. 'So you'll share more of yourself with me from now on?'

Share his whole life with her if she was willing to accept it. But there was no need to rush. Better not to. She might be wary of making a commitment for life after her experience with Haynes. He wanted her to be very, very sure of it.

He smiled. 'What are doing for Christmas this year?'

CHAPTER FIFTEEN

Christmas at Gundamurra…

KATHRYN knew it was a big step in her relationship
with Mitch Tyler—being invited to the outback sheep
station where he had 'done time' with Ric Donato and
Johnny Ellis. All three of them were here now, with
Ric also bringing Lara and their baby son who'd been
named Patrick, honouring the man who still stood tall
in their lives.

Patrick Maguire…the strong, caring father none of
them had ever had, and Kathryn noted he treated them
as much valued sons; welcomed into his home, listened to, enjoyed for the people they were, given respect for what they'd done and were doing with their
lives. It was clear that Lara also felt a bond with him,
having spent three months at Gundamurra after her
escape from her husband.

Kathryn was the only *outsider*. Not that she wasn't
warmly welcomed. She was. But the others were
clearly at home in this world unto itself, and she
wanted to feel that, too, feel part of it as they did.

Maybe she needed more time here to take it in, to
understand the unique rhythm of the place which, after three days, was already seeping into her—the
sense of there being no hurry to do anything, that the
endless land around them would wait timelessly for

footprints upon it, that the universe above with its brilliant blanket of stars would still be there, night after night.

No hurry.

Space for breathing.

Time to think.

And Kathryn found herself thinking a lot about where she was in her life and what she wanted in her future.

Patrick's three daughters were amazing people. Jessie, the eldest, had just signed up with the Royal Flying Doctor Service, based in Alice Springs. Emily, who loved flying, was a helicopter pilot. Megan, the youngest, had just come home from an agricultural college, determined on helping her father run Gundamurra. They each had real purpose in their lives and their energy for what they'd chosen shone out of them.

Kathryn felt pale in comparison, just as she had with Harriet Lowell. Her own career had not really been planned. It had been more a series of steps, each one satisfying her for a time before moving on to something else. Her position with Ric was as an assistant, not a driving force. She had no great personal ambition although she was certainly capable of doing whatever she set out to do. Was she lacking in something important? Did Mitch find her lacking?

Had he brought her to Gundamurra to find it?

This concern was playing through her mind on the day before Christmas. Everyone was busy with preparations. All the women were in the kitchen which was a hive of industry. Mitch and Ric and Johnny were putting fairy lights around the trees in the court-yard. Kathryn was surprised when Patrick Maguire drew her out of all the general activity, claiming he was too old for Christmas chores and wanted her company.

'Mitch tells me you play chess. Come and give me a game, Kathryn,' he invited.

He walked her along the verandah to the other side of the quadrangle courtyard which the huge home-stead enclosed, and ushered her into his office. Even though they were in the outback, a satellite dish linked them to all modern technology and the office looked very much the hub of business with computers and every other up-to-date aid. However, set beside a window between the desks at one end and the filing cabinets at the other, was a chess table, chairs on ei-ther side, the pieces set up ready to play.

It struck Kathryn as odd that it wasn't in the games room, along with the billiard table and the sound sys-tem Johnny had installed, plus shelves loaded with boxes of board games that clearly provided plenty of home entertainment. She wondered if chess filled lonely hours for Patrick Maguire since his wife had died and his daughters had been away, pursuing what they wanted to do.

'Did you teach Mitch to play?' she asked as they sat down at the table.

He smiled. 'No, my dear. He taught me.'

'You took the time to learn from him?' It seemed extraordinary to Kathryn—a man of his age learning from a boy of sixteen.

'It helped me understand the power of his mind.

And it is, without a doubt, the most formidable mind I've ever been challenged by. Even when he was sixteen,' he added in soft reminiscence, his eyes scanning hers as though gently probing for her understanding of it.

She smiled, speaking her own experience of Mitch. 'He cuts through all the greys and goes straight to the core of any issue.'

'Black and white,' the old man remarked, nodding thoughtfully. Then he asked, 'Does that trouble you, Kathryn?'

She shook her head. 'Not at all. I like it. He has a system of values that I feel very secure with.'

He nodded. 'When they first came here—the three boys—I asked them what they would most like to have that would make their time at Gundamurra better for them. Ric chose a camera, Johnny a guitar. Both items indicated an individual bent that was special to their natures—Ric with the vision to see and capture so much, Johnny with his love of music. But Mitch chose a chess set. Which I thought odd, because to me, it was a game that required two players. He said he could challenge himself, playing both sides.'

'You didn't believe him? Is that why you learnt?'

'No. I believed him. But it struck me he was used to being alone, living in his mind, fighting his own battles. And he'd ended up here because he didn't have the tools to take on the world by himself at the time. Learning chess gave me the time to talk about that with him. And to take some of the loneliness away.'

She looked at him appreciatively. 'You're a very remarkable person, Patrick.'

He smiled. 'They were three very remarkable boys. The most gifted of all who came through here. I always think of them as the three Ps—the passion of Ric, the pleasure of Johnny, and the power of Mitch.'

'The power...yes.' She smiled back. 'It was the first thing that struck me about him.'

'He's a warrior. Always will be. That's Mitch's nature. And the battle-ground he's chosen can be very lonely, Kathryn.'

It sounded like a warning. 'He's not alone with me, Patrick,' she assured him, certain of that in her own mind. 'And I very much support his fight to deliver justice.'

'I was thinking more...' He paused, cocking his head on one side, viewing her curiously. 'What would you have chosen, if you'd been one of the three?'

'Probably a sketch-book,' she answered without hesitation. 'I trained as a graphic artist. Part of why Ric chose me as his executive assistant. He thinks I have a good eye for the best shots.'

'But you're not ambitious for yourself?'

She sighed. 'Is that a terrible flaw in me?'

He laughed. 'We can't all be burning lights. How could they keep burning without a support system? Never underestimate the importance of support, Kathryn. An assistant who cares and shares...whose support one can always trust...there is a huge need for people like that...the nurturers of this world.'

*The nurturers of this world...*it suddenly struck Kathryn that was precisely what Patrick Maguire was—a man who had nurtured many burning lights. It was okay to assist. In fact, it was more than okay. It was a special gift in itself. Support one can always trust. Indeed, it *was* her nature to nurture. Just like her mother. Like Patrick. Except…there was one wrong note in all this…unless it could be explained.

'I noticed in the games room, you have copies of Ric's prize-winning photographs on the walls, and all of Johnny's music he's recorded…'

'But the chess table is here?'

'Yes. I just thought…well, there was nothing of Mitch in that room, and I wondered…'

'Where is he at Gundamurra?' Patrick tapped his forehead. 'In here, Kathryn. And this table is always set up ready for battle to be joined between us. We still play chess by correspondence.' He waved to the computers. 'By e-mail these days.'

'For lack of a handy partner,' she murmured, remembering Mitch's own words on their first night together.

'I'm glad he has you now, Kathryn.'

'And I'm glad he brought me to meet you, Patrick.' The man who had supported him all these years—the touching of minds that Mitch had needed, being known for who and what he was.

Ric and Johnny had shared that, too. Old friends. Special friends who understood what no-one else could without having had the experience here.

'You are very welcome, Kathryn,' Patrick said warmly. 'Very welcome.'

And she finally felt the bond—the knowing, the caring and the sharing—knew why Mitch had brought her here, why it was important to him. In a way, it was the ultimate gift of himself, the one deep insight that made sense of everything else, *if* she had the eyes to see it.

The knowing grey eyes of the old man who had seen so much were smiling at her, making her feel good about herself, good about being here with them all, reminding her what Mitch had said about the name, Gundamurra. In the Aboriginal language it meant 'good day'.

It was.

A very good day.

'Thank you, Patrick.'

He nodded and gestured to the chess pieces. 'Black or white?'

For the traditional Christmas carols session in the courtyard after dinner, Mitch had claimed the absolute centre of the lawn for him and Kathryn. They sat on the rug and cushions he'd set ready, surrounded by all the people who lived and worked on the outback sheep station. The pepper trees on the corners of the quadrangle were strung with masses of fairy lights and on the verandah facing them was a wonderfully decorated Christmas tree, under which lay Patrick's gifts for his staff and their families.

Johnny led them in the singing, playing his guitar like the virtuoso musician he was. Everyone joined in. He even had all the children marching around the courtyard to 'The Little Drummer Boy.' In between the carols, people wandered over to the verandah to fill their glasses from the keg of beer or the bowl of fruit punch, pick up a mince pie or a piece of Christmas cake. It was a very merry evening.

And Kathryn was thoroughly enjoying it, joining in, happily chatting to all and sundry as though she finally felt she fitted in here, and now saw Gundamurra as the special place it was to Mitch. He didn't know what had been said between her and Patrick over their game of chess this afternoon, but her beautiful green eyes had been shining ever since, shooting their magic sparks at him, making his heart dance with joy.

At first he'd worried that it might have been a mistake to bring her—too much to handle with Ric and Johnny here, too. Johnny, in particular, could be overwhelming company. And Patrick's daughters were no shy violets, either, always brimming with positive purpose.

These past three days, Kathryn had been sticking closely to Lara, with whom she obviously felt an empathy. But something had changed this afternoon. He sensed that whatever questions had weighed on her mind—and heart—had been answered and she was happy with the answers.

Which surely meant he could proceed with confidence.

It was simply a matter of choosing the right moment.

The carols were interrupted for Patrick to give his Christmas speech and hand out the gifts. He wore a Santa Claus cap and declared he was standing in for Santa because the kangaroos pulling the sleigh weren't hopping fast enough and wouldn't reach the outback until after midnight. Kathryn laughed and reached out to Mitch, taking his hand and squeezing it.

'He's a wonderful old man,' she said fervently.

'He is, indeed,' Mitch agreed.

'I think it was a very lucky choice…your coming here to him, Mitch. For Ric and Johnny, too.'

'You won't find any argument on that from any of us, Kathryn.'

'Thank you for sharing all this with me. It's very, very special.'

'I'm glad you find it so.'

More than glad. So much more it was impossible to put into words. It was like being reborn into a world where peace and well-being reigned. No dark shadows. No uncertainties. Pure pleasure.

They listened to Patrick, watched him having a personal word with everyone who accepted a gift from him. When that ceremony was over, they joined in a rousing chorus of 'We Wish you a Merry Christmas,' and finally a quieter, but no less feeling rendition of 'Silent Night.'

The station families trailed off to their own homes.

Patrick's *family* cleared away what needed to be taken inside, cleaning and tidying everything, ready for tomorrow. Mitch had deliberately left his rug and cushions on the lawn, and as everyone else was drifting off to bed, he steered Kathryn back outside, insisting it was a night to watch the stars for a while.

They lay together on the rug, looking up at a universe that seemed to be twinkling just for them. For Mitch, it had been a long journey to this moment, but he had no doubts about the decision hovering in his mind. It felt right now. Completely right.

'It's magic, isn't it?' Kathryn murmured, awed by the beauty of the outback night.

'Yes. But for me, the real magic is down here.'

He rolled onto his side, propped himself up on his elbow. She smiled at him. He was tempted to kiss her, but he didn't. Her answer would mean more, coming without any physical persuasion.

'Will you marry me, Kathryn?'

'Yes.' No hesitation. Not the slightest second thought. Her eyes engaged his very directly, serious now, yet glowing with an inner light that touched his soul. 'I love you, Mitch Tyler. And I now know what love is.'

'So do I. It's what I feel for you. Will you wear my ring, Kathryn?'

'Yes. For the rest of my life, Mitch.'

He took the small box out of his pocket, opened it, extracted the ring he'd chosen for her and slid it onto the third finger of her left hand. She lifted her arm to see it and the fairy lights in the trees sparkled through the deep green of the centrepiece which was set in gold and surrounded by star-like diamonds.

'An emerald…' It was a sigh of pleasure, drifting into a smile that transmitted her whole-hearted pleasure in him. 'I've always loved green.'

Then her arm lifted higher, curling around his neck, pulling him down. They kissed, pouring their love out to each other, and to Mitch the whole world felt green, like spring arriving, with all the promise of a vibrant new life taking over from a long, long winter.

His and Kathryn's life…together.

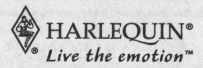

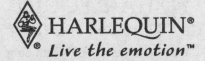

If you enjoyed what you just read,
then we've got an offer you can't resist!

Take 2 bestselling love stories FREE!

Plus get a FREE surprise gift!

Clip this page and mail it to Harlequin Reader Service®

IN U.S.A.	IN CANADA
3010 Walden Ave.	P.O. Box 609
P.O. Box 1867	Fort Erie, Ontario
Buffalo, N.Y. 14240-1867	L2A 5X3

YES! Please send me 2 free Harlequin Presents® novels and my free surprise gift. After receiving them, if I don't wish to receive anymore, I can return the shipping statement marked cancel. If I don't cancel, I will receive 6 brand-new novels every month, before they're available in stores! In the U.S.A., bill me at the bargain price of $3.80 plus 25¢ shipping & handling per book and applicable sales tax, if any*. In Canada, bill me at the bargain price of $4.47 plus 25¢ shipping & handling per book and applicable taxes**. That's the complete price and a savings of at least 10% off the cover prices—what a great deal! I understand that accepting the 2 free books and gift places me under no obligation ever to buy any books. I can always return a shipment and cancel at any time. Even if I never buy another book from Harlequin, the 2 free books and gift are mine to keep forever.

106 HDN DZ7Y
306 HDN DZ7Z

Name	(PLEASE PRINT)	
Address	Apt.#	
City	State/Prov.	Zip/Postal Code

* Terms and prices subject to change without notice. Sales tax applicable in N.Y.
** Canadian residents will be charged applicable provincial taxes and GST.
  All orders subject to approval. Offer limited to one per household and not valid to current Harlequin Presents® subscribers.
  ® are registered trademarks owned and used by the trademark owner and or its licensee.

PRES04   ©2004 Harlequin Enterprises Limited